# CONTRACTED COWBOY

## Quinn Valley Ranch, Book 1

# LIZ ISAACSON

ISBN-13: 978-1638761235

# CHAPTER ONE

"Oh, we'll need two jars of pickled beets from the cellar." Granny Gertrude pointed one aged finger with a slight bend in it to Georgia's list.

Georgia Quinn admired the wrinkled skin and paper-soft quality of her grandmother's hands. She looked up into her bright blue eyes, still as mischievous as ever.

"Doesn't Gramps hate beets?" Georgia asked, making the one next to the beets on her list into a two.

"Oh, he loves them." Granny waved her hand like she was swatting at an annoying fly. "And when you go to the grocery store today, make sure you get several extra bags of chips. We always run out."

Georgia changed the four to an eight on her shopping list, enjoying this quiet, peaceful time with her grandmother.

Yes, she hated the Quinn family parties and get-togethers. There seemed to be an endless string of them, as if something as trivial as Flag Day or the First Day of Fall required a huge shindig with the people she saw nearly everyday anyway.

But the annual Harvest Festival was something she thought should be celebrated, because it meant a tremendous amount of work had just been completed on the family ranch where she and her siblings lived and worked.

"Are eight bags enough?" she asked. "It's just us, Granny." The larger Quinn family got together from time to time, including at the Fourth of July, Thanksgiving, and just before Christmas. She wasn't sure if they were all as crazy as her branch of the tree and had celebrations for things like a full moon, but it didn't matter.

Georgia had been dreading the upcoming holiday get-togethers in all their varieties for a few months now. Maybe since last New Year's Day when her long-time boyfriend, Simon Flower, had broken up with her instead of popping the question.

She frowned at the mere thought of Simon. She hadn't been on a date since, and he'd been out with three different women in the last nine and half months. She shook her head, her long auburn hair brushing her arms as she did. But the thoughts wouldn't go.

"Eight is fine," Granny said, moving into the kitchen to put on the kettle. "Do you want tea?"

"Have I ever not wanted tea?" Georgia grinned at her grandmother. "How have you put up with all these family events for so many years?"

Granny Gertrude smiled back at her, the weathered, wonderful expression of someone much wiser than Georgia looking back at her. "Oh, honey." She got down two teacups, and Georgia thought that might be it. Granny was getting up there in years, and she sometimes lost her train of thought in the middle of the railway.

She put the cups on the counter where they'd been going over the grocery list for the Harvest Festival. Georgia would go and get everything she could that night, and the day before the big event next Saturday, the four sisters in her family would spend all day making the food for the cowboys, ranch hands, seasonal workers, and anyone else who had come to help them put in their cattle and crops.

Georgia was tired just thinking about it.

Granny sat at the counter and twirled her teacup. "I don't mind the family parties. When you're my age, they're something to look forward to." She gave Georgia a look with loads of sparkle in her eyes. Georgia sometimes got in trouble after Granny looked at her like that.

"What?" she asked.

"You just need a boyfriend," Granny said, and Georgia almost rolled her eyes. "Then the parties are more fun."

"Okay, Granny," Georgia said, chuckling as the tea kettle sang. "I'll get right on that."

THAT EVENING, SHE WAITED AS LONG AS SHE COULD TO GO into town. It was a twenty-minute drive from the ranch where she lived, and if it were later at night, there was less chance of her A) seeing someone she knew, and B) getting sucked into a conversation about her lackluster love life she didn't want to have.

After all, the grocery store in Quinn Valley wasn't one of those big chain, open-twenty-four-hours type of stores. She'd only gotten a cart and put in five jugs of apple juice from a display just inside the door when someone said, "Hello, Georgia."

That voice.

She turned as the creepy-crawlies started up her spine. Sure enough, Simon himself stood there, looking all debonair with his dark hair swept to the side. Honestly, Georgia thought he'd always tried too hard to look like Hollywood's next big thing, when really he'd left Quinn Valley for less time than she had.

"Hello, Simon," she said as nicely as she could.

"Shopping for the Harvest Festival?"

"Yes." She glanced at a woman who came to Simon's side. She was the model type, with a bigger gap between her thighs than humanly possible. Georgia instantly felt inferior, though she probably only carried an extra ten pounds, and Simon had always told her it was in the best places anyway.

"This is Carrie," he said, as if Georgia hadn't been in the same class as the other woman for many years. He really was so arrogant.

"Hey, Carrie," Georgia said, consulting her list. "I have to—"

"Darling, we should get going. We'll be late to the movie." Carrie gave Georgia a slightly wicked look as she tried to tug on Simon's arm.

"You look good," he said to Georgia, to which Carrie practically hissed.

"You guys go on," Georgia said in a voice that was much too loud. She worked to quiet it, when really she just wanted to rage at her stupid ex-boyfriend who hadn't had a problem moving on from their four-year relationship.

Four years.

And some of the best years of her life too. She couldn't believe she'd wasted them on him. Hadn't seen his inability to commit much sooner. She smiled as she said a prayer to maintain her composure.

"I have to meet my boyfriend later too, and this list is *long*." She waved the list at them as if they cared what was on it. Then she walked away, a new, strange idea morphing in her mind as she searched for the crushed tomatoes her mother would use to make the most amazing tortellini soup.

The next morning, Georgia read and re-read the words she'd typed into the box on the computer screen. Quinn Valley had a small newspaper with poor circulation, but their online classifieds were huge. It wasn't really something run out of Quinn Valley, but Lewiston, which was about an hour away.

But if she wanted a car, a dog—or a job—everyone in the vicinity knew to check the online classifieds first.

And she was about to post a job for a handyman to help her finish the barn. She almost scoffed. She did not need help finishing that barn, except for maybe Father Time, who seemed to keep throwing tasks at her that prevented her from getting out to it to finish it.

She flexed her fingers and read the ad one more time. It sounded reasonable. She needed someone who was handy with a hammer to help on the Quinn Valley Ranch. She couldn't put *must be handsome*, or *men without girlfriends only* in the text.

She wasn't that desperate. At least she didn't think she was. And she would not be hiring this person to be a handyman around the ranch, but to be her fake boyfriend for the next three months as she faced the busiest time of year for Quinn family events.

Granny Gertrude *had* said they'd be more fun that way.

Georgia's guilt almost had her deleting the listing. She knew Granny hadn't meant for her to *hire* a boyfriend, but since the other options for finding a man hadn't panned out well for her, Georgia felt like her choices were a bit limited.

And the women at church had already twittered to her about her "new boyfriend," because word in Quinn Valley got around quickly, and apparently Carrie hadn't wasted any time in mentioning the fake beau to anyone who would listen.

Determined now to show her and Simon—and herself— that she'd moved on, Georgia hit CONFIRM on the listing and not one moment later, a message popped up that her listing would be live within the next fifteen minutes.

She sat back in her chair, her desk filled with folders and

notes that sat at precise ninety-degree angles. No one came in her office without her permission, and nothing happened at Quinn Valley Ranch that Georgia didn't know about. Didn't schedule. Didn't plan.

*You can't plan a boyfriend* her mother had said. Georgia knew that. She did. But maybe, just maybe, she could hire one.

A WEEK LATER, HER SITUATION WAS DESPERATE. SHE WASN'T sure what she'd been expecting. Maybe that within fifteen minutes, her phone would blow up with potential handymen —er, boyfriends—and she'd have her pick?

But it hadn't. In fact, only one man had applied. A Logan Locke, and she'd scheduled an interview with him that morning, which was seriously cutting it close as the Harvest Festival was the following evening.

But apparently, Logan had been on another job that didn't end until yesterday and he couldn't come until today.

"He's all you've got," Georgia told herself as she straightened her hair and then pulled the sides back. "So don't blow it. Don't apply your list of boyfriend rules to him. He doesn't need to meet them. He just needs to A) not have a girlfriend." She held up her fingers as she started checking off items. "B) not be a felon, and C) be able to pretend better than almost anyone."

She sighed and dropped her hands to the bathroom sink in front of her. "This is impossible." But she still turned, pulled on her cowgirl boots, and headed out of her bedroom.

All of the Quinns in her family lived on the ranch property somewhere. She and her three sisters shared the main homestead, which had seven bedrooms spanning two floors. There was a kitchen upstairs and down, the office where

Georgia maintained the operations on the ranch, a piano room where Jessie gave lessons when she wasn't dealing with the animal births, and four bathrooms.

Her parents had built a cottage in the corner of the yard and moved into it a few years ago. Her older brother, and the only boy in the family, Rhodes, lived in a cabin closer to the main road. He'd take over the ranch one day, and the homestead would become his. He'd said he wouldn't push any of his sisters out, but Georgia was hoping to be long gone before then.

He lived next door to her grandparents, and he took care of them a lot of the time. Georgia went down to their cabin several times a week as well, and she treasured her time with them. They didn't seem to care how close she was to getting married and having children, and she felt more peace there than almost anywhere else on the ranch.

There were cowboy cabins that sat in an octagon beyond the main ranch buildings, which included a dozen stables, several huge pastures for the horses, two bull pens, and three barns full of pigs, chickens, and even a wild turkey or two.

Behind the barns, a huge field with llamas and potbellied pigs and a couple of goats often found Georgia standing there, talking to the animals as if they could understand her. Today, those pigs and llamas were her goal. She'd named them all after explorers, some so obscure she had to give history lessons to some of the new cowboys who came to work the ranch.

A knocking in the unfinished barn caught her attention as she passed it. Her heart flopped in her chest like it had been hooked up to an electrical pulse. "Hello?" she called as she entered through the doorless entrance.

A man turned toward her, his dark gray cowboy hat going well with those bright, bright green eyes. Her heart wailed at her now, and her legs stopped working completely. He wore his beard neat and trim, just how Georgia liked.

He was mesmerizing, and Georgia forgot her own name for a moment. Then, it registered that he stood in her barn, with a hammer in his hand. *Her* hammer.

She stepped forward to take it from him. "Who are you?" she demanded. "And what are you doing in my barn?"

He let the hammer go without resistance, those eyes pulling at her and drinking her up and smiling like they'd just shared a funny moment. "I'm Logan Locke," he said swiping the sexy cowboy hat from his head to reveal gorgeous sandy blond hair. "I'm here to interview to help finish this barn."

Georgia let the hammer fall to her side. She couldn't have picked a more handsome fake boyfriend if she'd held a lineup of cowboys. And she knew her granny was about to be proven right. This holiday season was going to be the best one she'd had in all of her thirty-one-years on Earth.

"Oh," she managed to say. "I'm Georgia Quinn. Some of my interview questions will seem a bit unconventional...." She wanted to reach up and tuck her hair behind her ear, maybe give him a flirty smile. But she kept her professionalism front and center. After all, she had to prove to him that she could pretend as well as he could.

"I'm ready," he said, tucking his hands in his pockets and giving her a smile that should be illegal. "Fire away."

# CHAPTER TWO

*L*ogan gazed evenly at the beautiful redhead, hoping she didn't noticed the way his jeans frayed along the cuffs and that his jacket was in need of several deep clean washes. He'd been flitting from ranch to ranch around the area this summer, and he was tired.

But he needed the money, and if this woman needed her barn fixed, he knew how to swing a hammer. It would pay rent and put food on the table, and Logan had enough experience on ranches to almost always get the job.

So let her ask her questions.

"First, do you have a girlfriend?" She pulled out her phone and focused on it, as if she really had typed that question into her interview list.

Surprise tugged at Logan's eyebrows, and they went up. He hurried to put his cowboy hat on, his main line of defense against pretty women. "Not at the moment. I mean, what does that have to do with building a barn?"

"I don't need any distractions," she practically barked at him.

Logan almost started laughing. Georgia possessed some

serious fire, and Logan didn't mind getting burned. He had a feeling she could really char him, though, so he kept his distance and waited for the next bizarre question.

"Are you available through the end of the year?"

He glanced up into the rafters of the barn. "There's no way this will take three months to finish. Maybe a couple of weeks." He met her eye again, and he had the inexplicable urge to step forward. But her glare and straight lips held him fast in place.

"Yes, ma'am," he said. "I'm available until the end of the year."

She consulted her phone. "Have you ever been in a play?"

"A play?"

"Like, the theater." She looked at him expectantly.

He had no idea what kind of questions these were. "No," he said slowly. "Look, I grew up on a potato farm that goes over the border between Quinn Valley and Franklin County. My youngest brother is going to inherit that, but all three of us boys grew up there, farming and raising animals." He indicated the barn. "I can finish this, easy."

Georgia looked at him, her eyes shooting hazel-colored lasers at him. She had a smattering of freckles across her nose and cheeks that he wanted to touch and then kiss. He was startled at the thought, and actually fell back a step.

What kind of thinking was that? He'd never met this woman before, and she hadn't been very friendly.

All at once, the fire left her body, causing her shoulders to slump. "Look," she said, glancing at the hammer still clutched in her hand. She set it down on the workbench where he'd picked it up. "I'll be honest with you."

"You haven't been?"

"Sort of."

Logan's stomach clenched, and his gaze flickered to the doorway he'd walked through. There was no door there. No way for her to lock him in. She wore jeans, a burnt orange T-shirt with a maple leaf on the front of it, and cowgirl boots. He was pretty sure he could outrun her if he had to.

But something kept him in place. Maybe idiocy. Maybe curiosity.

She looked like she was working up the courage to tell him what was really going on. Her mouth opened, and then she snapped it shut again. He edged toward the door, keeping the temporary workbench between them.

"Maybe I should just go," he said. Though he needed the money, he did not need crazy, and there were other ranches to find work. None as beautiful, as big, and as perfect as Quinn Valley Ranch. If he could get on here permanently, his whole outlook on life would change. His opportunities would be endless.

But there really were other ranches.

"How good are you with meeting new people?" she asked, a bit of desperation in her eyes now. Logan knew the look; he saw it every morning in his own expression.

"I'm...okay," he said. "Why? Georgia—ma'am—what is going on here?"

"I don't need your help with the barn," she blurted. "I can do that myself." She took a long, deep breath while Logan's hopes of getting on at this ranch in any capacity faded to a distant dot on the horizon.

"Oh."

"I need someone to be my boyfriend for the next three months." Her eyes slid down to his cowboy boots—probably noting how he'd glued patches back together—and back to his eyes. "What do you think?"

Logan had no idea what to think. He took another step toward the door. "I—I have no idea what's going on here."

She moved sideways too, positioning herself between him and the wide open exit. "Look, the Quinn family is like, the biggest clan in the valley, right?" Her face screwed up in disgust, and she sounded like she'd rather have a different surname.

"Yeah," he said slowly.

"Well, we have a lot of events between now and New Year's. I don't want to go alone. I'd be hiring you to go with me."

"Georgia!"

She spun toward the door at the sound of the male voice calling her name. Relief painted Logan's insides when her older brother appeared in the doorway. Rhodes, who was the same age as Logan's thirty-six, stood there. He looked back and forth between Georgia and Logan.

"Oh," he said, clearly taken aback by finding Logan there. "What's going on?"

"I'm hiring him to fix this barn," Georgia said without looking away from Logan. Oh, so she was fairly decent at telling little white lies. And he wasn't so stupid that he couldn't see the edge of desperation in her gaze. That edge that said, *Please, please, Logan. Go along with it.*

"Hiring him?" Rhodes asked, his gaze stuck on the side of his sister's face. "Georgia, we're done with the seasonal workers."

She finally tore her eyes from Logan's and looked at Rhodes. "I'll pay him from the admin budget. I can't get to this barn, and it's driving me nuts that it's not done."

That at least sounded true.

"We don't have budget for the barn," Rhodes said, obviously still confused.

Logan felt like a fool, standing there while they talked about the job right in front of him.

"Then I'll pay him from my check," Georgia said. "I'll handle it, Rhodes." She turned fully toward him. "What do you need?"

"Betsy wants to see you." He hooked his thumb over his shoulder. "I was on my way out to the bull pens and said I'd see if you were talking to the pigs." He flicked his eyes to Logan, and his whole face turned bright red. "I mean—"

Georgia drew in another breath, and Logan didn't want to be around when that particular tactic stopped working. Oh, no, he did not. "I'll be in soon," she said. "Tell her I'll be there at nine-thirty, like we agreed."

"All right." Rhodes backed out of the barn, turned, and practically ran away.

Georgia faced him, her own face a shade of red that Logan actually found quite attractive on her. "I do not talk to the pigs."

"Of course not," he said. "Now dogs. You can talk to dogs. It's like they know what you're saying." He clamped his mouth shut. What was he doing? He had no idea, only that he didn't want her to feel self-conscious.

She lifted her chin. "You have my number. I think I've made the job quite clear. Any questions, text me." Georgia started for the doorway, and she'd just stepped through when a question popped into Logan's head.

"When does the job start?" he called after her.

She twisted and looked at him over her shoulder, those half-green, half-brown eyes calling to him even across a couple dozen feet. "Tomorrow night. Our annual Harvest Festival includes my whole family, and every employee who helped with the harvest. Probably fifty people."

He nodded and said, "I'll let you know by morning."

She walked away, leaving him to stand in the nicest barn in the county, wondering what in the world he'd gotten himself into. Well, not yet, but he had the very dangerous thought that he would be telling the beautiful Georgia Quinn that he could probably pretend well enough to be her boyfriend for a few months.

Probably.

"HOW'D THE INTERVIEW GO?" KNOX KICKED OFF HIS BOOTS at the back door, an old habit from their childhood, because their mother didn't like dirty boots mucking up her clean house.

"It was...interesting," Logan said. "And before I left, I talked to a guy in their horse stables."

"Oh?"

"They're looking for a farrier. I told them about you. He took your number."

"What was his name?" Knox pulled out his phone and continued into the house where Logan lived with his twin. It was smack dab in the middle of Quinn Valley, everything he needed within a twenty minute drive—including that white whale of a ranch to the north.

"Rhodes," he said, looking at Knox like he'd lost his mind too. Honestly, had Logan entered the Twilight Zone and not known it? "You know Rhodes."

"Oh, well, yeah. You said 'a guy.' I thought it might be someone else."

Logan was tired, and he hadn't even worked that day. But if there was one thing more demoralizing than any other, it was looking for work. "Sorry," he said.

"So the interview didn't go well."

Georgia hadn't mentioned that he couldn't tell anyone about their arrangement. But it felt like that was an unspoken rule. Quinn Valley might have fifteen thousand people, but in a lot of ways, it felt like everyone knew everyone else's business.

"It went okay," he said. "I think I'll get the job." All he had to do was text her and say he'd take it.

"When will you know?"

"Tomorrow morning," he said.

Knox's phone chimed, and he looked down at it. "It's Rhodes." He grinned as he looked at his brother. "Maybe we'll both get a job out at that ranch. Wouldn't that be something?"

"It sure would." Logan busied himself with heating up a couple of bowls of soup they'd brought home from the farm over the weekend while Knox started having quite the text conversation with Rhodes Quinn.

With dinner hot, and Knox grinning like he'd won the Idaho lottery, Logan pulled out his own phone and typed out a text to Georgia.

*I'm in. Should we meet before the party to get some details straight?*

He stared at the words, thinking he was absolutely insane to even be considering the woman's offer. She'd lured him out to that ranch under false pretenses. Asked him all kinds of crazy questions. Proposed something absolutely unthinkable.

Then he thought about her pretty face and that expansive and expensive barn. That ranch. If he could get the experience at a ranch that big—and keep a job for a few months— he might have a shot at buying his own cattle operation in the near future.

He hit send and flipped his phone over before picking up his spoon.

He hadn't even taken a bite when his device vibrated. Logan couldn't help it; he looked at the message.

It was from Georgia and very short. *9 AM. The barn. See you tomorrow.*

He grinned at his brother. "I just got the job."

"Great." He showed Logan his phone. "I got an interview too."

"Amazing." He picked up his spoon again, a simple prayer

of thanks running through his mind. Maybe God had led him out to Quinn Valley Ranch for a different reason than finishing a barn. Maybe he'd been able to open the door for Knox to get a job. Maybe he could help Georgia weather the holiday season—which was obviously rough for her.

*Whatever it is,* he prayed. *Let me be successful in doing it.*

After all, he wanted to keep the job at Quinn Valley Ranch too.

# CHAPTER THREE

Georgia's heart felt like someone had encased it in cement when it was constricted, so now that it was trying to beat normally, it kept banging into sharp edges and rigid walls. She worked in the kitchen upstairs with Jessie and Granny Gertrude, while Betsy, Cami, and her mother manned the one downstairs. It was all hands on deck to get all the food ready for the Harvest Festival.

At least Betsy, the self-proclaimed chef of the family, was downstairs. Then Georgia didn't have to listen to how she was crimping the pie dough wrong on the apple turnovers. Instead, she got to listen to Jessie sing in her gorgeous soprano voice, a song about lost love on the range.

Granny hummed too, her gnarled fingers some of the best at making the baked ham and cheese sandwiches they had every single year. It was simple really, with hamburger buns, ham slices and Swiss cheese. But the sauce was a family secret, and Georgia wasn't even sure how to make it yet. She knew it had poppy seeds and butter, but there was something else in it too. Granny had brought a vat of it from her cabin, so Georgia hadn't seen her make it.

Her stomach fluttered at the thought of Logan's text. He'd taken the job, and a smile spread her lips now the same way it had last night. She couldn't believe it, but she'd been praying all morning that she could sneak out to the barn to meet with him for a few minutes come nine o'clock.

A timer went off, and she practically jumped out of her skin. Even with floury fingers, she reached for her phone to silence it, noting that Jessie had quieted too. She wore her reddish-blonde hair shorter than Georgia, and she cast her sister a look.

"What's that for?" The oven clicked, something it did from time to time for no reason. So it was still on, and the apple turnovers inside had twenty more minutes.

"I need to check on Columbus," she said. "He was having a hard time last night." She wiped her hands on her apron and stepped over to the sink, hoping the little white lie wouldn't cost her too many points with the Lord.

The potbellied pig *had* eaten too much last night, and Georgia had found him lying on his side near the fence. So it wasn't exactly a lie.

"Those have twenty minutes left," she said, nodding toward the oven timer as she suds-up her hands. "I should be back by then. If I'm not, this tray is ready to go." She skipped drying her hands in an effort to get out of the homestead more quickly.

"Seems like she's sneaking off," Granny said, but Georgia ignored her. Behind her, Jessie giggled and said something to their grandmother. Georgia didn't care what they thought. They were up to their elbows in food prep, and neither of them would come looking for her.

She hurried down the back steps and across the lawn, the scent of baking bread from the basement kitchen meeting her nose. As soon as she stepped from grass to gravel, the smells of the ranch returned. More horse than yeast. More cow than savory ham. More sweat than sugar.

Ducking into the unfinished barn, she expected to see Logan already standing there, just like yesterday. But it was empty. She looked at her phone, and sure enough, she was a few minutes late. Which meant so was he.

Annoyance sang through her. Didn't he get how important this was? They'd start the masquerade that afternoon. She turned and checked outside again, lifting her phone to her ear as she stepped over to the pasture where the pigs and llamas grazed.

Before the call could connect, he said, "Hey, sorry I'm late."

She jumped away from him, her heart pounding against that encasing inside her chest. "You scared me."

He was just as handsome today as yesterday, and she thanked God one more time for this good fortune in her life.

"Sorry, I couldn't find anywhere to park."

"Yeah, the Harvest Festival is today," she said. "Everyone's on-site already."

"Maybe we should start with what the Harvest Festival is," he said.

Georgia explained it quickly, and then she said, "So we need a story about how we met. Because our relationship is so new, I think that's all we'll get asked today."

"There will be a lot of people here. Who'll be asking?"

"Mostly my parents and my siblings," she said. "Maybe Granny." Gramps didn't usually get involved in the romantic things happening around the ranch. Heck, Georgia didn't either. But no one else in her family was seeing anyone right now, so a new boyfriend would be big news at the Quinn Family picnic table.

"All right." He blew out his breath and leaned against the fence as Magellan the llama came closer.

"Magellan bites," Georgia said. "I'd back up a bit."

Logan looked at her like she'd spoken Japanese, and she nodded to the llama. "That's Magellan. He bites."

Logan danced away from the fence, surprise on his face. "Interesting name."

"They're all explorers," she said. "The pigs and llamas, at least. I didn't name the goats, and we only have two anyway."

Logan looked like he had no idea what to say, and Georgia cursed herself for exposing her eccentricities so soon in their relationship.

Then she had to remind herself that this was *not* a real relationship.

She gazed out into the pasture too, wishing a nicer llama had come over so she could pat it and take some comfort from its soft summer hair. Instead, she got the grumpy face of Magellan who would spit if Georgia even so much as twitched toward him.

"What about an online story?" she asked. "I mean, we did meet online. It wouldn't be a complete lie."

"In like, an online dating...thing?"

At least he seemed as unfamiliar with Internet dating as she did. "You know what? I've heard of that app—Soulmates.-com? What about that?"

"I've heard of that," he said.

"So we met on the app," she said. "And we've been having so much fun getting to know each other that we've decided to meet in person." In the distance she saw Columbus, the dark brown potbellied pig, waddling toward her. So he was okay. "Sound okay?" She flicked a look at Logan, not wanting to look right at him again.

Number one, he was so handsome, it hurt. Number two, she didn't need to explain about the explorers right now. Number three, she was sure her embarrassment showed in her face like a bad sunburn—something else that happened to her frequently without the proper sunscreen usage.

Then her freckles popped out and her eyes looked more watery than normal. They were already the color of the duck pond behind the garden, and she didn't need them to be even murkier than they already were. So she kept her eyes on the slow-approaching pig.

"So if we've been chatting online, shouldn't we know a little something about each other?" he asked.

Georgia opened her mouth to start listing her favorites, but her phone alarm sounded. She jumped and said, "I'll text you, okay? I have to get back to the kitchen."

She made the mistake of looking into his green-like-summer-grass eyes, and the whole world stopped. Somewhere outside the two of them, her alarm continued to sound. She breathed, but only because it was involuntary.

The air smelled like lightning had just struck, and she wondered if the weather had turned so quickly. It was known to do so in Quinn Valley, and they'd have to relocate the Harvest Festival.

He smiled, and Georgia had never seen anything so beautiful in her whole life. His mouth moved, and she jerked again. She'd have to get an appointment with Raina if she kept up with all the jumping and being startled. Maybe she should get a massage anyway. Georgia certainly felt wound tight.

*It's just the Harvest Festival*, she told herself as she fumbled to silence her alarm. She wasn't sure what Logan had said, so she ducked her head and said, "The Festival starts at three. Can you be there?"

"Yes," he said, the word finally having sound in Georgia's ears. "Did you need help with the setup or preparation or anything?"

"Oh, I'm sure we do," she said. "Rhodes is in charge of the huge tent, and I don't see it up yet."

"So I'll go find him."

"Sure," Georgia said.

"And you'll text me all those things I'm supposed to know about you."

"Yep." She stepped past him and hurried back to the homestead. It wasn't until she turned the corner and put a physical structure between her and Logan that she could breathe properly again.

"You're in so much trouble," she whispered to herself. What had she been thinking? She couldn't even breathe around the man. How was she supposed to take him to family functions and act like they knew each other?

She was used to flaunting her boyfriends at family events, and as she crossed the lawn and hurried up the back steps, she knew what she needed to do.

Flaunt him.

She pulled her hair out of its ponytail and pushed into the house.

"There you are," Jessie said. "I was just about to send out a search party."

Georgia put a big smile on her face. "Sorry. I got…distracted."

"By a pig?" Jessie indicated the empty tray. "That needs to be full in twenty-five minutes."

Georgia stepped over to the sink and washed her hands again. "Not by a pig. By a man." Those words got Jessie and Granny Gertrude to stop their work in the kitchen. It was so quiet that Georgia could've whispered and they'd have heard her.

The oven clicked.

"Who is it?" Granny asked, her blue eyes so keen now.

"Logan Locke?" Georgia said like it was a question. "It's

brand new, but I invited him to the Harvest Festival just now. He's gone to find Rhodes and help set up." She returned to her bowl of dough and started rolling again.

"Logan Locke," Jessie said. "I don't know him."

"Doesn't he have a brother who's a farrier?" Granny asked. "I think we've had a Locke out here before."

"Yes," Georgia said, though she wasn't sure. "I can't remember his name though."

Her phone buzzed in her pocket, but she was up to her wrists in turnover dough, and she'd have to rush to fill the tray as it was. Logan—at least Georgia hoped it was Logan—could wait.

GEORGIA COULDN'T GET TO THE PHONE FOR AN HOUR, AND even then, she had to text from the bathroom. *Do you have a brother who's a farrier?*

Then she scanned his list of favorites. *Food: steak.* How unoriginal.

*Color: blue, like the sky. Okay.*

*Music: country.* Very cowboy, and not at all surprising.

Then he'd said he was from a potato farm on the Quinn Valley border but lived in town now. He was a seasonal ranch worker, looking for a permanent position, and yes, his brother —Knox—was a farrier. He had another brother, that was younger than he and Knox.

*So you're a twin?* she sent.

*Yep. I'm the older of the two.*

*I have three sisters and a brother. I'm smack dab in the middle of them all.* Georgia couldn't dictate her distaste, so she just sent the words.

*I'm the same age as your brother,* Logan sent. *I knew him growing up.*

Georgia wasn't sure if she liked that little tidbit or not. Rhodes was a great guy, but he could also see and hear a lie pretty easily. He had to when he worked with cowboys all the time. He'd definitely be their biggest challenge, and Georgia told Logan that.

*All right,* he messaged. *Oh, and I volunteer at the Customer Appreciation event at the hot springs every year, and I've always wanted to ride in a hot air balloon.*

Georgia smiled at the message. Logan seemed like he had a good heart, and she wondered why he'd agreed to be her fake boyfriend for the next three months.

She tapped out the question and hesitated. What if she didn't like the answer?

*Better to know his motivation,* she told herself and hit send.

*Honestly?*

*I think we should at least be honest with each other,* she told him.

*I need the money,* he said. *It's a job, right? I need the work.*

Georgia's heart pinched, and she sent Logan a list of her favorites, some things she wanted to do in her life she hadn't done yet and flushed the toilet though she hadn't used it.

Armed with a bit more knowledge, Georgia's confidence that she could pull off this ruse bloomed. When she returned to the kitchen, Jessie caught her eye.

"What are you smiling about?" her sister asked.

"Nothing," Georgia said in a singsong voice, just the way she would've had she really had a new boyfriend to show off later that day.

She started on the next item—a batch of cookie dough brownies—while Jessie ran downstairs to get the bottled peaches for the pie she was supposed to make.

Granny Gertrude leaned into the counter and said, "So you got yourself a boyfriend for the holidays."

"I mean, maybe," Georgia said, trying to downplay the

relationship and avoid Granny's eyes at the same time. "It's brand new, Granny. I don't know if it'll last that long."

"Well, at least the Harvest Festival will be more fun, right?" Her eyes positively gleamed before she moved over to the fridge and pulled out a huge jar of mayo. "Okay, I think I'm on potato salad next."

# CHAPTER FOUR

*A*fter hiding out in the unfinished barn, waiting for Georgia to text, Logan finally got some of the answers he needed and went in search of Rhodes. Logan caught sight of his twin from several feet away. He laughed with Rhodes Quinn near one of the stables, and Logan decided now was as good a time as any to see if there was anything he could do to help get the Harvest Festival set up. After all, Knox would make an easy buffer.

Anxiety hit him hard when he realized he'd have to play the part of Georgia's boyfriend in front of his brother. His *twin* brother, who knew everything about him, right down to the fact that he hadn't spent the last few weeks texting the beautiful Georgia Quinn and that he'd never heard of Soulmates.com.

Logan's feet grew roots, and he couldn't force himself to take another step. When Knox glanced his way and saw him, he gestured to Logan and said something to Rhodes. Well, there was nothing to be done now. He somehow got his feet moving forward and he shook Rhodes's hand.

"You're out here again?" Rhodes asked.

"Yeah," Logan said, exchanging a look with his brother. "Your sister hired me."

Rhodes narrowed his eyes, and Logan felt sure he'd be able to see right through the façade, just as Georgia had said. "I can't believe she needs help with that barn."

Logan shifted his feet. "Yeah." He cleared his throat. "She said you might need help with the set up for the Harvest Festival today?"

"Yeah, of course." Rhodes started walking down the road in front of the stables. "I've got men out getting chairs and tables from the church, but we can get everyone together to start on the tent."

Logan wondered if he should say anything. After all, would he be expected to stay for the meal if he helped set up a tent? Should he just blurt out that he and Georgia were dating? He felt like every step he took was on brittle earth, and the next one would shatter the ground and he'd fall through.

The next one...the next one....

But the ground held, and his mind swirled, and he stayed silent. Knox had no problem chatting things up with Rhodes, and they got in the front two seats of an all-terrain vehicle that seated six.

Logan was content to ride in the back. Always content to just hang out for a while, see what was happening. At least that was what his father said, and why he claimed Logan wouldn't be able to run his own ranch.

He pushed away the toxic words. Quinn Valley Ranch was beautiful, and as they drove down the dirt road to a grouping of cabins, Logan let the wind try to steal his cowboy hat and kept a prayer going behind his tongue.

"Cowboy lodging is out here," Rhodes said. "Your job as farrier doesn't come with room and board." He looked at Knox, his eyes holding an edge. "Is that okay?"

"Oh, yeah. Logan and I have a place in town," Knox looked at his brother. "And I wouldn't be here full-time anyway."

"I do need you a few days a week." Rhodes parked and got out of the ATV. "That's okay? You can fit us in around your other ranches?"

"I sure can." Knox beamed at him.

"Great." Rhodes seemed to relax a bit. He went on to detail that they had sixteen cowboys working for them, in various jobs from general horse care to working with bulls to the farming side of things. "My sisters do a lot too," he said. "So let's get 'em out and get that tent set up."

He walked over to a flag pole in the middle of the ring of cabins and rang a bell Logan hadn't even seen. It took a few minutes, but all the cowboys came spilling out of their cabins to report for duty.

"We need to get a fifty-foot tent set up," Rhodes said to them. "Let's get 'er done." He walked back to the ATV like he expected the men to know where to go and what to do. Logan was a bit surprised that they actually seemed to.

He could hardly believe that he and Rhodes were the same age, and he wondered if maybe he had been letting life pass him by a little bit. He watched the clouds in the sky, how they drifted, and he didn't want to do that anymore.

*So don't*, he told himself as Rhodes parked and indicated a huge white tarp spread out in the grass behind the homestead. The back door on the cottage in the corner opened, and an older gentleman came out. Rhodes's father.

Logan hadn't been best of buddies with Rhodes, but everyone knew Harvey Quinn. Everyone knew all of the Quinn's. Logan kept his head down and worked hard, hoping that maybe after he and Georgia ended their fake relationship, he'd be able to get a job at the ranch the way Knox had.

BY THE TIME THREE O'CLOCK CAME AROUND, LOGAN WAS ready to head home for an afternoon nap. Instead, he found himself walking up the steps of the homestead and ringing the doorbell. Georgia had texted him and asked him to do so, and well, it was part of the job.

She opened the door and let out a blessed blast of air conditioning, and Logan sighed. "It's hot for this late in October," he said, taking off his hat and fanning his face.

"Supposed to cool down by Monday," she said with a grin. She cocked her hip and leaned it into the doorframe. "Do you really like country music?"

"You really don't?" He could throw a tease right back at her if that was what she wanted.

"And steak?"

"What? Steak is delicious. It's better than pepperoni pizza. I mean, we're not in elementary school anymore, you know?" He thought maybe he'd crossed the line, but then Georgia's face broke into a smile and she laughed.

"I know I'm simple." She sobered and looked at him. "That's okay, isn't it?"

"Sure," he said easily. "I mean, put meat in front of me, and I'm happy. It's okay that your favorite food is also the favorite of eight-year-olds nationwide." He grinned at her, somewhat surprised at how easy she was to talk to.

She'd freaked him out in the barn during their first meeting, and their second had shown him a less animated version of the woman he'd met yesterday. A more subdued version.

"Are you ready?" she asked.

"Yes." He shifted back half a step. "So, what? Are we holding hands out there? We won't have to you know...kiss or anything, right?"

"No," she said quickly. "No, we Quinns aren't the type to

be all affectionate in public." She actually shuddered, and Logan wondered why she'd chosen him.

She joined him on the porch, and he asked her. She froze and looked up into his eyes, pure panic in hers. All at once, he got it. "I'm the only one who applied to finish your barn." He didn't even have to phrase it as a question.

"Well...yes."

Logan squinted out into the horizon. He couldn't help feeling a little hurt. Then he remembered that strange, strong, electric surge from earlier that morning when their eyes had met. Had she felt it too? That had to be something, right?

Georgia led him down the steps, and then she paused. "I do think we should hold hands."

"Oh, all right." Logan licked his lips and swallowed. "It's, uh, been a while since I've done that."

Georgia looked at him like he'd sprouted a second head. "It's pretty easy, Logan." She slipped her hand into his, her palm flat against his. "See? Done."

Logan couldn't respond, because every cell in his body felt like it had just been ignited. Her hand felt perfect in his, with smooth skin and a slight chill.

"So tell me about the explorer names," he said.

Her grip tightened and then released. "It's just something I did when we got the pigs and llamas. We rescued them from a farm over in Lewiston that was being sold, and I thought they must be on a grand adventure." She sighed and looked out into the sky like she wished she could be on a grand adventure somewhere.

"So we have five potbellied pigs, and I named them Columbus, Marco Polo, Boone, Buzz, and Pinto."

Logan had heard of two of those people. He didn't want Georgia to think he was dumb, but he had to ask. "Boone and Buzz?"

"Daniel Boone and Buzz Aldrin."

"Ah, a space explorer. I bet that pig is so happy he's named after an astronaut."

Georgia laughed again, and Logan decided he liked the sound. Liked that he was the one eliciting it from her. Liked holding her hand. Liked it all.

"Is there an Armstrong in there?" he asked, also making a mental note that this was not a real date. He was not her real boyfriend. He couldn't allow himself to think so for even a moment.

"Oh, that's a llama," she said. "We have about a dozen of those."

"Hmm." They rounded the corner of the house, and Logan froze at the sight of the tent. At least two dozen people had already arrived at the festival, and he wasn't sure he should be one of them.

"It's going to be fine," Georgia coached, but her fingers had definitely increased in pressure on his and they weren't easing up.

So he took another step, and so did she, and before he knew it, they'd arrived under the tent too. He recognized a couple of her sisters, and he nodded at them. They abandoned what they were doing and came over to Georgia.

"Hey, guys," she said. "This is Logan Locke. Logan, this is my older sister Betsy, and my younger sister, Jessie." She glanced around. "I have another younger sister somewhere around here...."

"Cami went to get the ice," Jessie said, tucking her shorter curls behind her ear where they promptly bobbed back out. All of the sisters had hair in various shades of red, from dark almost brown like Georgia, to a lighter strawberry blonde like Jessie.

Betsy wore hers piled up in a messy bun and she squinted at Logan for a few moments past comfortable.

"Logan?" she asked, glancing around. "I swear I just saw you with Lars and Bentley...."

"Oh, that was probably Knox," he said. "He's my twin."

"There are two of you?" Betsy looked at him with extreme interest now. Her gaze switched to Georgia, and it seemed like an entire conversation happened without any words being spoken.

Logan knew, because he and Knox could do the same thing.

"Does Knox have a girlfriend?" Georgia asked, and Betsy let out a slow hiss. Logan looked back and forth between the two sisters, and then he burst out laughing.

He shook his head as he quieted. "No, Knox doesn't have a girlfriend."

"There you go," Georgia said, but Betsy wore a look of disgust, shook her head, and walked away.

"You better make sure Granny doesn't need help with the sandwiches," she called over her shoulder, and it was Georgia's turn to hiss.

"Granny." She twisted back to the homestead. "Come on, Mister Muscles. I'm going to need your help for a minute."

"No problem." Logan would rather be put to work, so he'd feel like he'd earned a daily wage. Because hanging out with Georgia was easy. In fact, it was enjoyable, and Logan could see himself very easily blurring the lines between professional and personal.

And that absolutely could not happen. Not if he wanted to take home a paycheck at the end of the day.

# CHAPTER FIVE

Georgia walked with Logan back to the homestead, the mood between them light and easy. Her mind had completely blanked now that they were alone, but she finally seized onto a topic.

"Do you like dogs?" she asked.

"Sure," he said. "I have two of 'em."

"What kind?"

"Oh, they're just mutts. Rutabaga—we call her Roo or Ruta—is some kind of hunting dog mix. And Mortie definitely has some lab in him."

She nodded, wishing she had a personal dog. "We have ranch dogs," she said. "But I kinda want one who follows me around while I work and sleeps with me at night."

"Is that so?" He gave her a curious look out of the corner of his eye. "My dogs are outside dogs. They don't get the soft bed."

"Poor things," she teased, climbing the steps to the back door. "Okay, so Granny will want to meet you. This will be a tricky meeting too."

"I'm sure it'll be fine." He seemed so relaxed, and Georgia marveled at that. She couldn't remember the last time she felt calm and peaceful, the way his handsome face appeared to be.

She opened the door and went inside, calling, "Granny? We're here to help with the sandwiches." Through the mudroom in the back and around the corner, Georgia went on into the kitchen.

Granny was just pulling a tray of double-layered sandwiches out of the oven. "Here you go, Harley," she said.

Gramps started grabbing the foil-wrapped bundles and tossing them into a bowl big enough to bathe a baby as if they weren't hot at all. He'd definitely done some blacksmithing around the ranch during his time, and Georgia wondered if he had any nerves left in his fingertips.

"Granny," she said. "Gramps." She stepped right next to Logan, who'd stopped a few feet behind her. "This is my new boyfriend, Logan Locke."

Both of her grandparents stopped what they were doing and looked at Georgia, and then Logan. Granny blinked but acted first. "Logan Locke. From the potato farm on the south edge of town?" She moved forward with the speed of a much younger woman. "I can see it is you. You have your daddy's eyes."

"Thank you, ma'am," Logan said, accepting her quick embrace.

"Harley, come meet Shipp's boy. You remember Shippy, don't you?" She waved at Gramps, and Georgia seized onto the name of Logan's dad. She couldn't believe she hadn't thought to ask that, but she could get a bit more information from him as soon as they were alone again.

"Of course," Gramps said, shaking Logan's hand. "Your family is good people. What are you doing these days?"

"Oh, uh." Logan cleared his throat. "Working around at

the valley ranches. I'm hoping to get one of my own someday."

Another piece of info Georgia should probably know about her boyfriend. She realized that she'd jumped into a deep pool, fully clothed, with no way to get back to the surface. She took a deep breath. It was okay. Fine. Granny and Gramps were smiling at Logan, and that was a good sign.

"Betsy might have a mental breakdown if we don't get these sandwiches out there," Georgia said. "So tell us what to do."

Granny took over then, giving directions as she was wont to do. Georgia handed Logan a pair of oven mitts, and they started moving sandwiches to fill the bigger bowls.

"Rhodes is coming," Georgia said, seeing her brother coming across the lawn. "He'll help you with this last box of sandwiches and get you across the uneven ground, okay?"

"All right," Granny said, and Georgia heaved the biggest bowl of sandwiches into Logan's arms.

"Let's go. Then Rhodes can hold the door for us." She loaded up her arms with more sandwiches, and they headed out. Several times as she went down the steps and across the lawn and then the field where the tables and tent had been set up, Georgia thought she might go down. But she managed to stay on her feet and put the sandwiches where Betsy indicated.

After that, things really picked up as more and more people arrived. Georgia slipped her hand into Logan's more for comfort than anything else, and surprise popped through her that this man she barely knew could provide that for her.

No matter what, Granny had been right. This family event was much better with a boyfriend, and Georgia put a smile on her face for her parents, her siblings, and everyone who worked the ranch.

She talked quietly with Logan, their heads bent together, as she learned the names of his parents—Shipp and Lucy. He told her more about the potato farm, more about his brothers, and more about himself.

"So no white meat during Thanksgiving, huh?" she asked.

"No, all the flavor is in the thighs."

"Fascinating." She really was fascinated by Logan, and she didn't have to work hard at pretending she liked him. She *did* like him. And the strangest thing was, he seemed to like her too.

*So let me get this straight. You've named all the llamas and pigs, but not the goats.*

Georgia smiled at the text from Logan. She'd practically worn her thumbs to the bone with how much they'd texted this past week. *That's right.*

*Why not? You think goats don't deserve to have names?*

*Fine,* she tapped out. *One's brown and one's white. Can I just call them Chocolate and Vanilla?*

*It would be better than nothing.*

She laughed softly in the privacy of her own bedroom, the soft morning light coming through her blinds. She hadn't gotten out of bed yet, and this kind of communication had become her new favorite.

*What are we doing today?* he asked her next, and Georgia sat up a little straighter against her mountain of pillows. They hadn't gotten together every day since the Harvest Festival, but only a couple of times. Once for lunch at the pub downtown, which had the best baked macaroni and cheese in the world, and once for a quick cup of coffee at Fresh Brew. She'd run into one of her cousins on the street, and it had been a bit awkward.

She, at least, had introduced Logan. Andrew had stood there uncomfortably, and Georgia wasn't sure what his girl-friend's name was. But she understood awkward, and Andrew was actually one of her more normal cousins.

*I have to work until five,* Logan's next text said.

Georgia didn't get off the ranch much, and Logan had picked up a job in town working on a home remodel the owners wanted done before the snow flew in Quinn Valley.

*What about working on the barn?* she suggested. *I did hire you to do that.*

*Sure,* he messaged back. *I'll come up to the ranch when I'm done in town.*

*Maybe I'll come down for tacos,* she sent. *I hear the taco truck will only do catering and to-go orders during the winter.*

*Let me know. I'll come meet you.*

And so Georgia got out of bed with a smile on her face, something that hadn't happened in a while. She showered, got dressed, and went into her office to see what she needed to get done that day.

Now that the harvest was finished, they just needed to get the cattle out of the hills. Rhodes had put together the crew to go get them, and he'd been gone for a couple of days. She didn't expect him or the cowboys back for another week probably, maybe longer. Then they'd have all their cattle in a central location for the winter, and the focus of the ranch shifted from outdoor things to indoor.

She found the paperwork for Knox's hiring on her desk, and she sat down at the computer to generate the forms she needed him to sign. Rhodes had considered going to farrier school himself, but he couldn't afford the time away from the ranch. Knox had recently completed the training, and he'd been working at three other ranches around the valley.

Georgia was glad Rhodes had hired him at almost the

same time she'd "hired" Logan, because then her new position didn't garner so much interest.

She completed that and then headed out, planning a stop at her grandparent's cabin before she went into town.

"Hello," she called as she opened the front door to their place. Her great-great-grandfather had built this cabin, and the three beside it, many years ago. It was affectionately known as Old Folks Row, as the Quinns who had dedicated their lives to the land and the family ranch lived in the cabins until they died.

A family cemetery lay about a hundred yards behind the line of cabins, and Georgia went there sometimes just to feel close to her family. Usually when she was lamenting that her last name was Quinn.

"There's just so many of us," she'd tell the headstones. "Don't you get tired of it all?"

Of course, they never answered back. But she definitely thought some of them would agree with her. The family stories said that the same great-great-grandfather who'd built these cabins didn't leave Quinn Valley Ranch for over two decades. He didn't like going into town, and he didn't like having people up to the ranch.

Things had changed over the years, as now all of Granny and Gramps's four children came to the ranch every Thanksgiving for a big, grateful meal together. They got together at other times of the year too—namely the Fourth of July and Christmas, though those events weren't held at the ranch.

But still, Georgia could see herself living on this ranch indefinitely, only going down to town to get groceries she couldn't grow herself.

That, of course, would never happen, as she wasn't going to inherit the ranch.

"Granny?" she called when she didn't see anyone in the living room or the kitchen at the back of the house. Down the hall were two bedrooms and two bathrooms, but she didn't hear any sound from that direction. She moved to the back door and looked through the window, immediately pushing the door open to go outside.

"There you are," she said, putting her hand on Gramps's shoulder as he sat in a rocking chair right beside the door. "She's tearing out the garden?"

"Yep, time for fall," he said in his wrinkled voice.

"I'm headed into town. Wondering if you guys need anything."

"I don't. Oh, yes, I do. I want some of that pistachio ice cream from the gas station. It's the only place you can find it."

Georgia grinned at her grandfather. "I'll get it for you." She moved down the few steps from the back deck and into the yard. "Granny," she called. "I'm going to town. Do you need anything?"

Her grandmother waved her gloved hands at Georgia and shook her head. "I'm fine, dear."

So Georgia went to town with two goals: tacos with Logan and pistachio ice cream.

LATER THAT DAY, WITH HER GRANDFATHER PROPERLY equipped with his treat, Georgia saw a red pickup parked near the chicken coops. It hadn't been there when she'd returned from her lunch date, and her pulse picked up instantly.

Logan unfolded himself from the cab of the truck, already wearing a smile. One exploded onto Georgia's face too, and she practically skipped over to him. "What are you doing here so soon?" They'd only had tacos together a couple of hours ago.

"Finished for the day." He reached for her hand though there wasn't anyone around to see. Georgia didn't mind—in fact, her gaze lingered on his mouth for an extra moment as her fantasies about what it would be like to kiss him bloomed to life in her mind.

"You said we could work on the barn."

"Oh, right." She started walking in that direction, a lightness in her step that could only be attributed to the man beside her.

"Do you like living on the ranch?" he asked, and the question sent a shiver of surprise through her.

"Yeah," she said. "I love the ranch."

"But you won't inherit it."

"No, but I can work here for a long time." She glanced at him. "Have you started looking for a ranch of your own?"

He laughed, but it didn't contain a lot of merriment. "No."

"Why not?"

He peered at her for a moment and then looked forward again. "Do you know how much ranches cost, Georgia?"

She had no idea, but she sure did like the way he said her name. A slip of foolishness heated her face as she shook her head.

"A lot," he said. "And I'm a seasonal worker, moving from job to job every chance I get."

Georgia swallowed, her mind racing for something to say. "That reminds me," she said a bit too loudly. "I have your first paycheck in my office. Let's make sure you don't forget it, okay?'

A frown marched across his handsome features before he said, "Okay."

"What was that look?" she asked.

"I don't know."

"Yes, you do." She paused in the middle of the path and

tugged her hand out of his. "Remember how we're honest with each other?"

He exhaled heavily and removed his cowboy hat to wipe along his forehead. "All right, then. I told Knox about us. About you hiring me to be your boyfriend, and he questioned if I should get paid for that. So I've been thinking about it."

Horror struck Georgia right beneath the ribs. "You told Knox about it?" She searched his face desperately, hoping and praying he'd say, *Just kidding! Of course I told no one about this insane deal we've made.*

"He already knew," Logan said. "Well, I mean, he knew I wasn't seeing you before the Harvest Festival. Knew I'd only been out to the ranch once for a job interview. He knows I've never been on a dating app." He gazed down the path, over her shoulder, and Georgia didn't like it one little bit.

"I had to tell him."

She shook her head and pressed her lips together. "Is he going to tell anyone else?"

"He said he wouldn't. We can trust him."

"And now you think I shouldn't pay you."

"I don't know what to think."

If Georgia were being honest with herself, she didn't either. "Well, you've done everything I've asked, and that deserves a paycheck. That's what I think."

His eyes found hers again, and that surge of electricity flowed freely between them. In one, swift movement, he swept her into his arms and held her against his chest. Every-thing inside Georgia tensed for one, two breaths, and then she melted into the strength of Logan Locke.

"All right, then," he whispered. As quickly as he'd embraced her, he stepped back, clearing his throat. "Let's go work on that barn."

Georgia walked beside him, every cell in her body alight

and burning with a new fire. And she knew she was treading on dangerous ground.

She was in very real danger of having the best holiday season of her life.

And in very real danger of losing her heart.

# CHAPTER SIX

*Do you ever feel like your life is just passing you by?*

Logan looked at the words on his phone and thought about them.

*Of course,* he sent back. *I'm thirty-six-years-old and have nothing to show for it. You, at least, have a ranch and all those llamas.*

His defense mechanism of playing things off as a joke had helped him through the last few weeks with Georgia. Every time he texted with her, every time he saw her, he felt like he was trying to climb a massive mountain of loose sand. He'd never reach the top, no matter how hard he tried, and he was constantly losing ground.

She was beautiful, and smart, and hardworking. She was easy to talk to, and had soft hands, and a good heart. If Logan had met her naturally, at the hot springs, or maybe as he threw a ball to his dogs in the park, he'd have gotten her number and done exactly what they did now.

Hold hands with her around the ranch. Grab coffee and chat. Eat tacos while the wind whipped around them, reminding them that it was almost winter in Quinn Valley.

Talk more than work in the barn, so that it was still unfinished.

And tonight, they were going to the Halloween Food Truck Rally, which drew out almost all fifteen thousand Quinn Valley residents. Not really, but it felt that way to Logan. Nothing from the trucks was worth waiting in line for a half an hour, but Georgia had been excited about going.

And what made Georgia happy made Logan happy.

He'd collected three checks from her, and it was the easiest work he'd ever done. Because it wasn't work. Sure, she'd been upset about him telling Knox about the true nature of their relationship, but even his brother had commented last night about how much happier Logan had been the last few weeks.

"You're not falling for her for real, are you?" Knox had asked, and Logan hadn't been able to vocally say no. So he'd shook his head, when really he wanted to nod. Confess to Knox, that yes, he had real feelings for Georgia.

*Speaking of llamas,* her text came back. *What are you going to be for Halloween tonight?*

Logan hated Halloween. His mother had never bought him a good costume growing up, so he'd always been left to piece together whatever he could. Going to school as a potato farmer or a bum was about what he could do, and he'd always been scoffed at or ignored. Which was honestly fine.

*Do I have to dress up?*

*It's Halloween,* she said, like that explained everything.

*I'll wear my cowboy hat,* he said.

*Oh, so you're one of those people.*

*Yes,* he said. *Whoever they are.* He'd slept less the last few weeks than he ever had, and he'd had to call the phone company and get unlimited texting for how much he and Georgia had been communicating. He hadn't seen her in a few days, and he just wanted to see *her*. Not some goblin or witch or bloody vampire.

*What are you going to dress up as?* he asked.

*Oh, I hate Halloween*, she said. His pulse skipped, and his heart expanded a couple of degrees. He and Georgia didn't have a ton in common, but enough to keep their conversations going. She was fiery where he was more laid back. She was by the book, everything lined up in ninety-degree angles, and he left his shoes by the back door wherever they fell.

She rose early and went to bed early, and Logan was a night owl. But they both liked coffee, and animals, and it seemed, each other.

And now, they both didn't like Halloween.

*I've never liked you more*, he typed out and stared at the words. Could he send them? What would she think? He'd held her hand plenty of times, and there had been that quick hug last week.... He was still thinking about holding her in his arms and how right it had felt. How she'd completed some part of him he hadn't known was incomplete.

In the end, he decided to send the text. If anything, it would give them something to talk about as they wandered the fair that night, searching for something that was less greasy than the booth beside it.

*See you tonight*, Georgia's text came in, and Logan sighed.

"What was that?" Knox asked as he came into the kitchen where Logan's cold cereal had gone soggy long ago.

"Nothing," he said, flipping his phone over. His brother saw the movement and lifted his eyebrows.

"Yeah, nothing named Georgia."

"Maybe." Logan got up and rinsed out the gross cereal. "Is it bad if I like her?"

"Of course not," Knox said, nodding to the refrigerator. "But you haven't cashed any of the checks she's given you." He didn't say anything else, because he didn't need to.

Guilt gutted Logan as he looked at the three slips of paper hanging on the fridge. "I'll talk to her about it."

"I mean, most women don't pay their real boyfriends to hang out with them."

"I know," Logan said, plucking his hat from the hook beside the fridge. "I have to go. I've got a job out near the hospital in Riston today. And Georgia and I are going to the Food Truck Rally tonight."

"I'll be there too," Knox said. "Maybe I'll see you."

Logan doubted it, what with how many people showed up to this thing, but he nodded and slipped out the back door. He threw the tennis ball for Roo and Mortie a few times, and then he got behind the wheel of his pickup.

He was good at construction, and he liked the way it made his muscles burn and bunch. Fitting things together and paying attention to every step he made on a rooftop kept his mind occupied so he couldn't think about Georgia.

All too soon, though, it was time to meet her at the Food Truck Rally, and he turned onto the street which housed the fairgrounds, where tonight's activities would take place. The event wasn't as big as the Eastern Idaho State Fair held in Blackfoot each year, but it would have little carnival games for the kids, and every food truck within a hundred mile radius had probably pulled in hours ago.

A Ferris wheel towered before him, along with a couple of other bigger rides typical of a small-town celebration. He parked down the block quite a ways, remembering the feel of an autumn night at the fairgrounds.

He pulled out his phone to send a message to Georgia. One thing they'd talked about was telling each other things as they remembered them, no matter when or where they were. He sent, *Just got here. Did you know I rode the rodeo circuit for a year? I don't think I told you that.*

*I did not know that. Meet me at the lemonade stand just inside the gates.*

After a brisk, ten-minute walk, Logan paid his ten bucks to get into the Food Truck Rally. The money went toward the candy parade the organizers would have later, as well as clean-up costs at the fairgrounds after tonight ended.

Logan spotted Georgia at the lemonade stand—and she wasn't alone. His heart beat a bit faster at the sight of her curves in those tight jeans and that black sweater with a bright yellow crescent moon on it, as well as the fact that it looked like he was about to meet another Quinn.

She'd managed to keep him away from them, claiming she wasn't overly fond of her last name. He still needed to ask her about that, but it hadn't come up in their chats yet.

"Hey, beautiful," he said, sweeping into her personal space and sliding one arm around her waist while he bent down and pressed his lips to her forehead. He drew in a deep breath, getting the floral, soapy scent of her hair, and then turned his attention to the other woman standing beside Georgia.

Logan grinned at her and extended his free hand. "I'm Logan Locke."

"Oh, so this is who Georgia's been hiding." She looked at Georgia with as many lights in her eyes as Christmas trees had. "You secret-keeper."

Georgia laughed and indicated the woman. "This is my cousin, Raina. She's a massage therapist, and she works miracles on my tired back."

"You have a hump," Raina said. "From sitting at that desk all the time."

"Raina," Georgia said in a teasing, warning voice. "Logan and I are still getting to know one another. Don't be telling him I'm a hunchback."

Logan laughed with the two women, and they started to walk through the rally. "What are we looking for tonight?" he asked. "Fried stuff? Desserts? Salads?" The Food Truck Rally really did have everything, including the famous taco truck that was a permanent part of Quinn Valley now.

"I want one of those all-in-one waffle things," Georgia said. "Have you heard of them?"

"Enlighten me," he said, his arm around her waist comfortable and shooting sparks down his spine with every step. Could she feel it too? Could she have real feelings for him? Or was she pretending because her cousin was with them?

*But what about all the times when you've been alone?* his mind whispered. All the texting. All the getting to know each other stuff. Was that all a ruse so the times when they needed to be a couple, it would seem like they really were?

"It's a waffle cone," she said. "Like an ice cream cone, but not sweet, and not so crispy. Then they put in fried popcorn chicken, mashed potatoes, corn, and cover it all with gravy. You eat it like an ice cream cone."

"I've had them," Raina said. "They're delicious. We have to find that truck."

Logan thought it sounded good too, but he was sure the line would be forever long at a place like that. Sure enough, several minutes later, they rounded a corner to a long line, and Georgia said, "There it is. Chicken Cones." She glanced up at Logan with a giddy expression on her face. "Let's get in line."

"All right," he said, smothering his sigh. After all, he hadn't had to dress up. His arm was still resting on Georgia's hip. And she was the most beautiful woman at the rally that night. He could wait in a line for a chicken cone if he had to.

An hour later, Raina had spotted someone she wanted to talk to, they'd gotten their all-in-one chicken dinners, and Logan was starting to wonder if he could kiss Georgia that night.

"So I have a question for you," he said to keep his mind on less imaginary things. "Why don't you like being a Quinn?"

He and Georgia walked slowly down one of the less busy rows, especially now that the main dinner time was over. The night bordered on the outer edge of cold, but the stars in the dark blanket of sky above them were beautiful.

"There's just a lot of us," she finally said. "And a lot of expectations."

He nodded. "Sometimes expectations aren't a bad thing."

"I know." She stepped in closer to him and laced her fingers through his. "I expected the holidays to be hard this year, because I've had a boyfriend for the past four years, but we broke up in January. So."

"Ah," Logan said, another piece of the puzzle fitting into place. "That's why you hired me."

"One of the reasons," she said. "Going to family things is easier for me when I don't have to worry about who I'm going to be sitting by, and if I'll want to talk to them. With a boyfriend, I know all of that."

"So you're a control freak," he teased.

She giggled but it only lasted a moment. "Yeah," she admitted. "I think I am."

"Better than a drifter, I suppose."

She took a couple of hurried steps in front of him and stopped. "Is that what you think you are?"

"I don't know." Logan gazed down at her, his thoughts scattering in a dozen different directions. "I like you, Georgia."

"I like you too, Logan."

"No, I mean—" He cleared his throat. "I haven't cashed any of the checks you've given me. I don't want you to pay me to be your boyfriend. I just want...to be your boyfriend." His mouth felt like he'd swallowed cotton. People walked by them on both sides, and he somehow couldn't hear anything outside of the bubble of him and her.

She blinked, her face one of perfect shock.

"Say something," he said, almost desperate for her to confirm that the feelings between them weren't one-sided.

"Georgia Quinn!" someone called, and the spell between them broke. She turned to look over her shoulder, and Logan's gaze followed hers to see who'd called her name.

She tucked herself into his side, muttering, "You're about to find out why I don't like being a Quinn." Then she said brightly for the whole world to hear, "Heya, Aunt April!" like she was the happiest woman in the world to see her aunt.

And Logan's confusion and frustration only grew. Because if Georgia could pretend that well, maybe everything between them had been a complete farce too.

## CHAPTER SEVEN

Georgia could've handled seeing almost any of the Quinns at the Food Truck Rally. But Aunt April? She was the family redneck witchdoctor, and that was not overstating it.

She rushed at Georgia, her long skirts flowing behind her the same way her red-from-a-bottle hair did. She gripped Georgia's face in both hands and kissed both cheeks, something that allowed the energy to flow properly. Or something. Georgia had stopped listening to Aunt April's stories about herbs and oils when she was six years old.

"I had a feeling I'd see you here tonight," her aunt said. "My gut, it never lies." Her gaze moved to Logan, and Georgia had the strangest urge to step in front of him as if he needed protection from her aunt.

"This is my boyfriend," she said, the words flowing evenly from her mouth. "Logan Locke."

"Logan. Locke." Aunt April said each name like it held the meaning to life's secrets. She shook his hand, grasping it and not letting go. She turned it over so she could study the lines there, and she said, "Oh, look at that."

Logan managed to get his hand back, and Georgia put a plastic smile on her face. "What are you doing here? Where's everyone else?" Aunt April did love her kids, and that branch of the Quinn Family seemed to do a lot together.

"Oh, they're off getting funnel cakes," she said. "I had the strangest urge to wander down this way. Now I know why." Her bright, beaming smile took up her whole face. "So tell me about you two. How long have you been dating? You didn't bring him to the summer picnic." She hooked her hand through Georgia's elbow, and she glanced at Logan.

His smile looked pained, and she almost started laughing. "Oh, Auntie. Let's save all the questions for the big dinner at Thanksgiving, okay? I promise Logan and I will sit by you."

"Big dinner at Thanksgiving?" Logan whispered, his breath cascading over Georgia's ear and neck, making her tremble with delight.

"Oh, there's Roxie. I have to run. So good to see you both." She kissed them both this time and ran off, leaving Logan looking like he'd just been hit with a dump truck.

"And that's my aunt," Georgia said. "There are several more where she came from."

"Wow," he said, still staring after her.

"Indeed." Georgia "So we obviously need to go over the calendar." She wanted to return to what he'd said before Aunt April had interrupted them, but she didn't know how. She couldn't just say, "I like you too, and hey, I'd love to be your real girlfriend."

Could she?"

"So there's the pie baking weekend coming up," she said. "It's traditionally the second weekend in November. All the women get together to bake the pies for the big Quinn Family Thanksgiving feast. It's held at the ranch every year, on Thanksgiving Day. We eat promptly at one o'clock. The men play turkey toss in the morning, and the afternoon is open for whatever."

"Turkey toss?"

"Literally, turkey toss," she said dryly. "My dad buys a few extra turkeys, and they go out in the snow and toss them around like footballs." She barely refrained from rolling her eyes. Perhaps Logan would like something like that. "They come in smelling like wet dogs and tracking snow and slush everywhere."

"Sounds interesting," he said, and she couldn't tell if he really thought that or not.

"We have the gingerbread house contest at Thanksgiving too," she said. "Everyone who wants to can build a house and put it on display in one of the cabins at the ranch. Throughout the weeks from Thanksgiving to the big family dinner in December, you go into the cabin and vote for your favorite house. No one in my family has won in years."

"Who wins?" he asked.

"Oh, Robyn's been taking home the blue ribbon for years. She's like this Pinterest queen, and she knows things about glue guns the rest of us have never heard of." Georgia laughed. "I actually like Robyn a lot. She's very talented."

"Oh, so your family isn't all bad."

"I never said they were *all bad*. I said sometimes the holidays can be hard with a million Quinns running around, vying for prizes and dinners and attention."

He brought her close to him, and Georgia went willingly. "So you want the prizes, the dinners, and the attention. Is that it?"

She gazed up into those gorgeous green eyes, falling into them for a moment. "Something like that," she said a bit breathlessly. Had he heard that in her voice?

"All right," he said. "I think I can make that happen for you this year."

How he was going to do that, she had no idea. All she knew was that she wanted him by her side for all the craziness ahead. And if that wasn't crazy, Georgia wasn't sure what was.

*ANY INSANE EXES IN YOUR PAST I NEED TO BE AWARE OF?* SHE sent the next morning before she got out of bed.

*Ha ha,* Logan messaged back. *I didn't date a whole lot. A girlfriend here and there. Nothing that serious. Nothing recent.*

She read over his text, her first feeling disbelief. Logan was drop-dead gorgeous, and the man could do almost anything with his hands. How did he not have a date every other night? Maybe for the same reason she hadn't been able to catch anyone's eye. Well, for her there were two reasons. She was a Quinn, and everyone in town knew her. Two, there weren't that many eyes to catch.

So how had she missed Logan all these years?

*Simon.*

The name was right there on the tip of her tongue, and she realized once again how much she'd lost because of her attachment to a man who wouldn't commit to her.

*What about you?* he asked, and Georgia should've seen the question coming. She took a deep breath and started tapping. Her thumbs flew across the screen as she told him about Simon and the four-year relationship that had left her contemplating becoming a nun.

*Well, I'm glad that didn't happen,* he sent, his response to the whole story somehow exactly right.

*Are you up for a long drive this weekend?* she sent him.

*I'm intrigued.*

She laughed quietly. *I have to go get all the cookies for the family plates. It's down in Utah, a little over an hour to this big cookie factory. Might be fun to go together.*

She hadn't planned on asking him to go with her. But she also hadn't planned on experiencing anything but frustration when dealing with the man she'd hired to basically be arm candy.

*I just want to be your real boyfriend.*

Georgia could still hear his words in her head, and she needed to let him know that was a real possibility. But an idea for how to tell him hadn't come to her yet. Perhaps a long drive together would spark something.

*Sure,* he said. *Are you driving?*

*Yep,* she said. *So tell me where to come pick you up.*

Georgia looked forward to her drive with Logan all week, and when she finally pulled up to the simple, two-story house in a quiet neighborhood, her nerves felt like someone had put them through a wood chipper.

His red pickup sat in the driveway, and as she got out, she pulled her purple parka tighter around her. It hadn't snowed yet, but the sky was threatening to do just that today.

From the back of the house, a dog barked, and Logan's laughter followed. Georgia paused to soak it in, because it was a wonderful sound that penetrated her heart and made her smile.

"Come on," he called, and the barking intensified. Bypassing the front door, she walked past the red truck and toward the back yard. She crept up so she could have a moment to observe him with his dogs. Her first view was of him bent over, scratching their heads while a bright orange ball sat at his feet.

He picked up the ball and both dogs sat at attention, the black one quivering with excitement. Logan launched the ball, and both dogs went after it.

"Mortie, let her get it!" Logan called, and Georgia remembered that he was the black dog. He did not let the smaller, brown dog get the ball, and galloped back to Logan with a huge doggy smile on his face.

She stepped, which shifted some dirt under her foot. The brown dog—Roo—looked her way, yipped and dashed right toward her.

Logan turned, and Georgia had half a second to meet his eyes before she had forty pounds of dog flesh in her face. "Hey, girl," she said, rubbing the dog's head and back. "Oh, you're just as fast as that Mortie, aren't you? Yes, you are. Yes, you are."

By then, Mortie had arrived, and he barked at her as he jumped up on her thighs. *Bark, bark.*

"Mortie," Logan said. "Four on the floor. Quiet."

Georgia had never seen a dog do exactly what someone said, exactly when they said it. But Mortie did. He whined as he settled on all four paws and sat. His tongue hung out of his mouth, but he didn't bark.

"Good boy," Logan said as he approached. The dog looked at him for approval, and Logan trailed his fingertips across the top of the dog's head.

He'd never been more attractive to Georgia, and his smile had never been more beautiful. Before he could take another step, she did, moving right into him and lifting both hands to cradle his face.

She caught a momentary look of surprise before she let her eyes drift closed and touched her mouth to his.

Fireworks exploded down her throat, and she suddenly wanted to stay welded to him forever. Their kiss deepened, and Georgia didn't mind one bit. She finally pulled away, her face on fire and the reasonable side of her catching up to what she'd just done.

The cold air felt good against her heated skin, and she glanced up at Logan, wondering how he'd take this new development.

"You're never paying me again," he whispered just before kissing her for a second time.

# CHAPTER EIGHT

*L*ogan had spoken true when he'd told Georgia he hadn't been in a serious relationship for a long time. As he kissed her, he realized he'd never been in a serious relationship period. Sure, he'd kissed other women, but it had never been like this.

This made his head swim. This made his heart hammer in his chest. This made him never want to kiss another woman.

Georgia giggled and ducked her head, giving Logan a moment to just breathe. He wasn't sure what he'd done to elicit such a wonderful thing from her, but he didn't care. He just wanted to kiss her again.

"So I guess you're not my pretend boyfriend anymore," she said.

"I'd really like that." He grinned at her.

"I have something else to confess," she said.

"Oh, boy. Lay it on me."

"I needed a new boyfriend to make my previous one jealous. He'd moved on already, and I hadn't, and I didn't want him to think that after ten months, I was still hung up on him." She finally lifted her gaze to his. "I'm sorry."

Logan looked into those beautiful eyes and held her close. "Are you still hung up on him?"

She cocked her head to the side as if she was really considering it. "You know what? I don't think I am."

Logan wasn't entirely convinced, but they were three weeks into their relationship. He could give her more time. "So we're driving for cookies today."

She startled and said, "Yes. Yes, we are. We better get going." She led him to her car, and he moved the seat back before he got in on the passenger side. His news felt like it might burst out of him, and he worked to keep it in until she had the car on the road, heading south.

"So, I looked at some ranches online this week," he said, trying to be ultra cool and casual.

Georgia sucked in a breath and then let out a little squeal. "You did? That's great, Logan. Tell me about them."

And because she was so easy to talk to, he did. "There's only two, and they're like, ten times smaller than Quinn Valley. But I think they're a size that I can manage on my own."

Georgia didn't immediately volunteer to help him run the ranch, though she'd said plenty of times that she did that for her family operation. He didn't really expect her to—well, maybe in his dreams.

"Cattle operations?" she asked.

"Yes, both of them. I haven't quite made the calls to see them yet."

"Why not?" She glanced at him and then back to the road as rain started to splash against the windshield. "Oh, it's going to snow today."

"I think you're right," he said. She didn't seem concerned, and she kept driving, so Logan didn't worry too much about it either. The weather had distracted her from why he hadn't made any phone calls about seeing the ranches he'd looked up online.

The truth was, he wasn't sure he could run a ranch. He'd never done it before, though he had worked almost every job there was. He wasn't sure he could qualify financially. He wasn't sure if Knox would want to go in on the ranch with him.

There were too many unknowns, and Logan had gotten overwhelmed pretty quickly. Just looking at the online listings had almost taken an act of God. He watched the wintery landscape go by in silence, wondering if Georgia liked winter outdoor activities. That seemed like a safe topic, so he asked her.

She groaned and shrugged. "I mean, we have a pond and I've been known to go out and ice skate. But other than that, I could do without the snow."

"So no skiing or sledding or anything."

She laughed and reached over to take his hand in hers. "I'm not sure if you know how old I am, Logan. No way I can get up and down on an inner tube and slide down a mountain. That's called insanity, and that's why little children do it." She giggled again, and Logan couldn't help joining in.

"Point taken."

"What about you? You enjoy winter sports?"

"Not really," he said. "It makes for a muddy construction site and not many jobs in the ranching world."

"And yet, we live in Idaho, where it snows for like, half the year." She shook her head, still chuckling.

"And we think children are insane," he said. "But I'd go ice skating with you."

"Yeah?" She glanced at him again. "I think I'd like that."

The rest of the drive was filled with easy talk about the family tree cutting ceremony, which he would be attending, of course. The Customer Appreciation event at the hot springs in December, where he volunteered every year. And how she really wanted a dog of her own.

Then they walked around a teeny tiny cookie store and put bag after bag of gingerbread men in their cart. Then a few more bags of sandwich cookies with chocolate in the middle. Some with mint. They probably had fifty bags of cookies by the time she declared they were done.

"What do we do with all of these?" he asked. He realized he'd said "we" as if he was part of her family holiday traditions, but the truth couldn't be more different.

"These are for the tree cutting," she said. "We serve tea, coffee, and hot chocolate with the cookies once we get back to the ranch. Then we all decorate the tree in the homestead, and go over to my grandparent's place, and decorate a smaller one there."

"That sounds nice," he said.

"It is nice," she agreed.

"So maybe you don't hate your family traditions."

"No," she said slowly as she started loading the cookies up onto the check-out counter. "I guess I don't."

"At least you have them," he said, helping her put the bags up where the cashier could see them.

"You don't have family traditions?" she asked.

"I mean, one or two. Stuff like putting up the tree the day after Thanksgiving. And opening a pair of pajamas on Christmas Eve. Of course, my family is much smaller than yours."

"Well, everyone's is," she said with a smile. She didn't seem like she cared that he was tradition-less, but Logan felt like he hadn't really started experiencing life until he'd met Georgia.

❄

ANOTHER WEEK PASSED, AND LOGAN COULDN'T WAIT TO SEE Georgia again. He'd kissed her outside his house again before she'd taken herself, her car, and all those cookies back to the ranch. But he hadn't seen her that week at all, because he'd been working on a construction crew that started at dawn and worked until dusk.

He was tired and muddy by the time he got home, and all he could do was throw the ball for the dogs a few times before hurrying in out of the cold and stumbling into the shower.

The force of texting was strong between them, but he wanted to see her. Hold her hand. Kiss her, kiss her, kiss her.

This Saturday, though, she was baking pies with her sisters, aunts, and cousins, and no one else was bringing a boyfriend. Or a male at all. So he'd been uninvited from the all-female pie baking marathon, but he could still show up at the ranch.

Knox would be out there working in the stables, and Logan had decided to tag along. He tossed his ice skates in the back of Knox's truck and climbed in the passenger side.

"Ready?" he asked.

"Yep."

Knox was one of those slow drivers, so it took almost a half an hour to get out to the ranch. He kept the radio on the country station, which satisfied Logan, and he hadn't said anything about Georgia or the paid boyfriend gig in over a week.

"Seeing Georgia today?" he asked as he pulled under the Quinn Valley Ranch sign.

"Yes," Logan said. "And you should know that she's not paying me anymore."

"Yeah, I figured," he said. "You ripped up those other checks, and I might have seen you kiss her last weekend."

Logan's pulse jumped over itself, but he wasn't embarrassed. "For the record, she kissed me first."

"So that wasn't the first time." Knox chuckled. "Nice, Logan."

"What? It's a mutual thing. She likes me, hard as that might be to believe."

"It's not hard to believe," Knox said, looking at him and not the road. "Why would that be hard for me to believe?"

"Nothing," Logan said, though his answer didn't really fit the question. His twin had always had more success with the girls, and Logan had always felt overshadowed. He'd never told Knox that—never told anyone—and he wasn't going to start now.

"I've got my eye on someone," Knox said.

"Oh, boy," Logan said with a grin. "Is that all I get?"

"Yes, because you'll mess it up for me."

Logan watched his brother, who suddenly needed to study the parking spaces like there weren't a dozen in front of the stables where he'd be working. "Where could you possibly have met a woman?" he asked. Knox worked on ranches, and they were primarily staffed by men. The brothers went to church together, but they'd never had any success with converting a woman there into a girlfriend.

So who had caught his eye?

He parked and got out of the truck—a little too quickly in Logan's opinion—and went into the stable without waiting for his brother. All at once, Logan knew who it had to be.

One of Georgia's sisters. There were three of them out here, all single. So which one was it?

He didn't ask but tried to be as helpful as possible while Knox worked on the shoes for the horses in several of the stables. Hours later, Georgia finally joined them, a hint of cinnamon about her.

"Hey, there," he said with a smile. He drew her into his arms and faced his brother. "I'm going to go, okay?"

"Yeah, go," Knox said, hardly looking up. Logan couldn't be sure, but he thought his twin's face was a bit flushed, but that could've been from all the hammering.

A dry snow fell outside, and Logan stopped by Knox's truck to grab his skates. "How far is this pond?"

"Oh, we're not walking," she said, nodding toward the ATV parked beside the truck. "It's not far, but there's way too much snow for that."

It had been dumping on Quinn Valley, and it was especially deep out here at the ranch, because they were higher in the hills.

She got behind the wheel of the ATV, and Logan sat in the front seat this time. It almost seemed too cold to be outside, but they arrived at the pond and put on their skates. As soon as he got moving around a bit, his muscles warmed up.

Georgia could skate much better than he could, and he fumbled around like it was the first time he'd put on blades. They laughed, the snow fell, and Logan wondered if he was falling in love with her the same way the flakes drifted to the ground.

She glided toward him and grabbed onto his shoulders, giggling. "You're not bad, cowboy."

"Are you kidding?" he asked with a chuckle. "I'm terrible." But he sure did like holding her in his arms, their bodies creating a bubble of heat in the chilly atmosphere. He gazed down at her, tilting his head down to kiss her. He'd never been happier to have answered a help wanted ad.

He hadn't seen any weird Quinn family drama yet, but the biggest activities were still to come. Logan decided he didn't care. If he had the opportunity to kiss Georgia, he could deal with a little drama.

# CHAPTER NINE

Georgia left the kitchen to Granny and Betsy, where they had a dozen other hands to help them get the Thanksgiving meal on the table.

Or rather, tables, as the homestead didn't have a big enough space for a single table that would seat every Quinn coming to dinner. There were thirty people just with Granny and Gramps's kids and grandkids, and the family was expanding seemingly every moment. Some Quinns had kids, like her cousin Heather, who hadn't been seen in the Valley for years. Georgia had heard she was back, but she hadn't seen her yet, and she didn't think Heather would be at the meal that afternoon.

She worked with Alyssa and Robyn, setting up tables in the dining room, the living room, and all the way to the piano near the front door. Then came the chairs, the silverware, the napkins, and all the glasses. It was seriously a lot of work to get ready to feed over forty people.

"Now we head to Granny's," she said. They didn't really go to Granny and Gramps's, but to the last cabin in the row of four. Georgia had put tables there a couple of days ago, and now they just needed to be unfolded. "You're okay to come, Alyssa?"

"Yeah, Jeremiah's out tossing that turkey around." She rolled her eyes like the turkey toss was a bit dumb, and Georgia couldn't agree more. They headed down the road to the cabin and she and her cousins started setting up the tables.

"So, you and Logan seem to be getting along," Alyssa said as she flipped out the legs on one folding table.

"Yeah," Georgia said with a smile, glad she didn't have to pretend to like him, or worry about what she might not know about him.

"I heard he didn't date," Robyn said.

Georgia wasn't sure what to say. "Well, he obviously does."

"After his last girlfriend—what was her name?" Robyn and Alyssa exchanged a look, and since they worked together so much, with many of Quinn Valley's residents, they probably heard a lot more gossip around town than Georgia did.

"Carol?" Alyssa guessed.

"Caroline?" Robyn tried.

"Something like that." Alyssa helped lift the table, and Georgia had the strangest urge to toss it at her. "Anyway, I'd heard that when she left town, she took Logan's heart with her. He hasn't dated since, and it's been years."

That didn't really mesh with what he'd told her, but Georgia couldn't let it bother her. Gossip was just that, and she'd rather rely on firsthand knowledge than what her cousins had heard years ago.

Sure, it bothered her, but she focused on getting the gingerbread tables set up, the papers for names and numbers by the door, and that she'd make it back to the homestead before the turkey toss ended.

Logan had come out for the festivities, and she wanted to be there when he came in. The men were still in the yard when she pulled up to the homestead, and relief ran through her. The homestead was warm inside—almost too warm—and she took a moment beside the front door to just breathe.

The different branches of the family had already started to congregate in specific locations, and she saw a face she'd seen only once. The dark-haired woman sat next to Georgia's cousin, Andrew, and Gramps, and she must be Andrew's girlfriend. Georgia searched for the woman's name in her memory, and finally just edged closer to the group until she heard Rachel.

Rachel. Not that her cousin, Andrew, had mentioned his girlfriend's name when she and Logan had bumped into them coming out of Fresh Brew. But now he'd brought her to a big family party. Good for him.

Before she could go into the kitchen to see what Betsy needed from her, the front door banged open and all the men came in, including the youngest little man in the Quinn family, Alyssa's son Jeremiah. The noise level doubled, and Georgia made a mental note of another thing she disliked about these huge family gatherings. Logan joined her, and she leaned into his touch, though it was absolutely freezing and her shiver had everything to do with temperature.

Logan seemed to thrive on the noise in the homestead, and he grinned around at everyone. She wanted to ask him about his ex-girlfriend, and if it was true he'd given her his heart. Because if so, maybe he didn't have it in him to love someone else.

Georgia couldn't believe she was even thinking about falling in love.

She shook her head and focused on Jessie, who had started singing in her high soprano voice. Ivy, another Quinn cousin who worked at the downtown restaurant as a server and part-time entertainer, stepped beside her and added her voice to Jessie's.

The impromptu concert caught everyone's attention, and even Georgia found herself smiling. "I bet your family isn't crazy like this," she said to Logan.

"Georgia, this is so much better than what's going on at my parents'."

"Really?"

He looked at her. "I suppose you should come meet them. Then you'll see. Thanksgiving is about eight people, because my uncle drives over from Lewiston. Sometimes we go there. He has one daughter, and once she got married, she only comes sometimes. So it's a bunch of men sitting around, talking about potatoes and potato farming, while my mother and my aunt put together a few dishes."

He watched as a huge, flat pan of mashed potatoes went by. "This is great."

As Georgia looked around at her family, she felt the spirit of them. Experienced the love they had for each other, even if they didn't always get along perfectly. The homestead was full of people, sure. Full of noise. Full of laughter, and love, and a touching spirit of goodness.

Georgia put her arm around Logan's waist and just held onto him, glad he'd helped her see what she'd been missing all this time.

"Time to eat," Betsy yelled, and Rhodes added an ear-splitting whistle to get everyone's attention. He nodded at Betsy, who smiled back at him. "Welcome to the ranch," she said. "Gramps wants to say something."

Their grandfather shuffled through the crowd until he stood beside the island, which was probably groaning under the weight of all the food piled on it. "Gingerbread houses must be in place by midnight tonight. The food is ready, and Gertie and I are so grateful for each of you in our family."

He paused, his throat working against his emotion.

Georgia felt that same spirit from earlier, and she found her own feelings swirling and storming through her.

"Thank you for coming. I've asked Bob to say grace." He nodded at Georgia's uncle, who stepped forward. After the prayer, the noise level exploded again, this time mostly with Betsy calling out the names of all the foods on the counter.

She and Logan edged through the line behind Cami, and they all sat together. Alyssa, Jeremiah, and Robyn sat across from them at the table closest to the door, and Rhodes and a couple of cowboys who didn't have family in the area took up the end of the table.

"Where's Knox?" Rhodes asked Logan, who'd just taken a bite of his turkey drumstick.

He chewed and swallowed, then said, "He's at my parent's today."

"Oh, that's too bad. Betsy was asking about him."

Logan whipped his head back toward the kitchen, and when he reached back to rub his neck, Georgia wasn't surprised. "What?" she asked.

Logan bent his head toward her and whispered that his brother had said someone had caught his eye. "It has to be her, right?" he asked.

Georgia's chest fluttered a little. "Maybe. I'll see what I can covertly find out."

THE NEXT MORNING, GEORGIA STOOD IN FRONT OF THE tables and tables of gingerbread houses. Robyn's was absolutely perfect, of course. She even had wispy marshmallow smoke coming out of the chimney, which poked out of a rooftop that looked like real shingles. Georgia even wanted to pluck off one of the candies and make sure it was, indeed, edible.

Because that was a rule. Every piece of the display had to be edible, except the board the house sat on. Even that was practically perfect on Robyn's display.

"She's winning again," she said, sighing as she turned away from the houses. She was quite proud of hers, as she'd made the entire thing out of gingerbread men cookies. The house, the roof, even the trees in the yard. She'd broken them, filed them into the right shapes, and used perfectly white royal frosting to put it all together.

She couldn't vote for her own—another rule—but she wouldn't vote for Robyn either. Or maybe she would. She wasn't sure, and she didn't have to decide right now.

No, right now, she needed to be up at the homestead, getting the cookies onto platters for when they all returned from their trip into the forest to find two Christmas trees. She stepped out onto the porch of the cabin just as Logan's red pickup rumbled up the snow packed road, and she tried to wave him down.

But the man drove fast, and he didn't see her. He'd said nothing about the ranches he'd looked up, and it had been weeks. She'd sensed it was a sensitive subject, and she'd told herself to let him bring it up.

She'd been thinking more and more long-term, though she'd tried to stop herself. After all, she didn't need to be making a commitment to another man who didn't want to commit to her.

But her mind did its own thing sometimes, and she'd been thinking about where she and Logan might live should they get married. He currently lived with Knox, and she had a bedroom in a homestead she didn't own. Could they even afford their own place?

Could she keep working for the ranch? Would he keep moving from temp job to temp job? If he bought a ranch, she could see their future as clearly as anything. They'd run it together and be happy on their little patch of land in Idaho.

She shivered, her body's way of telling her to get out of the cold to daydream, and she hurried down the steps to her car. She followed Logan's pickup to the homestead and found him coming back down the steps.

"There you are." He kissed her hello, and she loved that such an action was so easy now, and still so wonderful. "Where is everyone? The house is empty."

"We meet at my parents' cottage. Come on." She led him up the steps, through the house, and out the back door. "They live back here." The sidewalk between the two dwellings was always kept clear, something Cami did religiously in the winter.

Sure enough, as soon as Georgia opened the door, she found her siblings and parents. Everyone wore their thick winter coats, hats, scarves, and gloves, completely ready to head out into the snowy wilderness.

"There they are," her mom said, giving her and Logan a fond smile. "Ready, everyone?"

Choruses of "Ready, Mom," filled the cottage, and Georgia went right back out the door she'd just come in. Around the corner of the house sat a few ATVs, and she got in the backseat of one, hoping she'd get Rhodes as a driver. Jessie could dump them out almost as easily as she could breathe, and thankfully, her dad took the wheel of her ATV.

"Hey, baby." Her mom reached back and patted her leg. "How do the gingerbread houses look?"

"Great," Georgia said brightly. "I have my favorites."

They started off then, and the crunch of snow under the tires, the wind, and the roaring engine made talking impossible. Logan took her hand and squeezed it. They exchanged a smile, and she snuggled into his side. The ATV didn't have a rear-view mirror, and she felt a little dangerous being affectionate in front of her parents.

Once out in the midst of all the pine trees, and after the sound of the engines had quieted, the resulting silence almost felt deafening.

"We need a small one for Granny," her father said. "And a big one for the homestead. Rhodes gets final say this year." With that, they set off through the snow.

"Rhodes gets final say?" Logan asked, still holding Georgia's hand.

"Yeah, that rotates," she said. "Let's just say that sometimes there's a fight over which tree to get. So every year, one of us gets final say."

"A fight? Wow. I think I'd like to see that."

Georgia laughed, the sense of wonder and peace out in these woods almost overwhelming. "When I was a kid, I used to love coming out here," she said. "It was so beautiful, with all the snow, and all the branches. Two colors. So simple." She drew in a deep breath through her nose, which almost hurt. "I love it."

"Mm." He swept a kiss along her forehead, along the bottom of her hat. "I can see why. It's beautiful. Serene."

"Serene," she echoed. That was the perfect way to describe it. "It feels like Christmas to me."

"Pine trees, and snow, and family. Definitely Christmas."

This year, there was no fighting among the siblings, almost like they all knew Logan wouldn't really want to see that, and they got the trees back to the homestead without any issues. Georgia let her sisters go ahead to get the hot drinks and cookies out, thoroughly enjoying having Logan with her and not having to stress about every little detail as she had in the past.

"Have you thought any more about getting a dog?" he asked.

"I mean, a little." She bent and picked up a handful of untouched snow, starting to pack it into a ball.

"I was thinking you'd like a bichon frise. They're these cute little dogs, and—" He cut off when the snowball struck him in the chest.

Georgia pealed out a lungful of laughter and started to run for the back door. Sure enough, a snowball struck her in the shoulder blades right when she reached the bottom step. She shrieked and nearly went down.

In the next moment, Logan caught up to her, laughing too, and pulled her back to the sidewalk. "You're nothing but trouble," he said between chuckles.

Georgia had never felt such happiness in her life. Not before Simon. Not when she was with Simon. Never. She reached up and touched Logan's cheek with her mittened hand, sobering the moment.

It felt like a moment to say *I love you, Logan*, but she couldn't get her voice to work. Thankfully, he kissed her, and somehow they both said what they needed to without speaking any words at all.

# CHAPTER TEN

*L*ogan enjoyed every moment of his time with Georgia—and her crazy Quinn family. He couldn't believe she didn't love their eccentricities, but the more he talked to her about it, the more he realized that she actually did.

The month of December was relatively quiet for the Quinns, and he went to work and prepped for the Customer Appreciation Day at the hot springs. He'd been volunteering since he was a teenager, and it was always a little intense when people got in for free. Especially if it had gotten cold early in the season, as it had this year.

He'd told Georgia he'd be at the hot springs most of the day, and she'd said that while she'd been a time or two, it wasn't a family tradition. She was, however, going to come so she could see him.

He liked that she really seemed to like him, and he was fairly certain that she wouldn't disappear in the middle of the night the way his last girlfriend had done.

Logan had actually been panicked when he'd found Carol Anne gone. Missing. Finally, a week after he'd gone by her apartment and found it cleaned out, she'd texted him to say she just couldn't keep pretending to like him.

He'd never been so hurt in all his life, and honestly, the next couple of years were kind of blurry in his memory. Even Knox had told him about some things he'd done that he simply couldn't remember.

Nothing terrible, but stuff he should be able to recall.

He pushed through the gate to enter the hot springs and joined the crowd of volunteers gathered around the check-in table. He'd wear a nametag the color hunters wore in the fall so anyone could identify him—and hopefully listen to him if he had to ask them to do something.

He'd get lunch at eleven-thirty, and he'd be done by four. Not only that, but he got a week's worth of free passes for the hot springs for anytime other than their special events. And Logan liked the hot springs after a long day building a house or laying cement or fixing a barn.

Whatever he had to do to make ends meet. As he waited in line for his assignment, he thought about the couple of ranches he'd looked at online all those weeks ago. He'd never done anything about them. The pages were still folded and in the top drawer of his nightstand. Knox didn't even know he'd been thinking about buying a ranch, and he should've told his brother first.

But now that Knox had the farrier job at Quinn Valley Ranch, he could afford the mortgage himself. It was only Logan that still hadn't found his path in life.

He pushed the thoughts aside and accepted his assignment to monitor the towel bins. He'd take in used towels to the laundry, and make sure there were fresh towels folded and available for patrons.

The hot springs were huge, with three pools of varying temperatures and sizes. The biggest and coolest was one hundred and two degrees, and most of the time it was full of families. The huge canopies kept things shady in the summer and free from rain and snow in the winter.

Open year round, the hot springs were the best during the winter months. They had heated decks to melt the snow, and the lights at night brought a smile to Logan's face every time he came. During Christmastime, the lights shone in an array of colors, but at most other times of the year, they were just red—like lava.

The premises weren't huge, but he got a partner to help with the towels. He didn't know anyone named Annie, which wasn't all that surprising given the number of volunteers there that day. People from all over would come to this free day at the hot springs, not just Quinn Valley residents, and as he left the volunteer tables, he searched the nametags for his towel partner.

He saw a woman standing beside the laundry door, her arms laden with towels, and he thought that had to be her.

"Let me help with those," he said, taking a huge chunk of the stack from her. Enough to uncover her face. He immediately dropped the towels, his heartbeat ricocheting around inside his chest.

"Carol Anne," he said, glancing down at her nametag, which read Annie.

But he'd recognize her face anywhere. It had haunted him for a few months after she'd left town.

"What are you doing here?"

She stooped to pick up the fallen towels. "I'm volunteering." She started folding them, but Logan would've just tossed them back into the laundry room. Guests didn't want a towel that had been dropped on the ground. "And I go by Annie now."

Logan had no idea what to say. He looked over his shoulder, thinking he should go get a new assignment. Even working the churro truck would be better than working with his ex-girlfriend for the next eight hours.

But the gates opened, and people began pouring into the facility though it was barely nine o'clock in the morning.

"Here," someone said, thrusting a stack of towels toward him. He had no choice but to take them, and he started toward the racks way over by the second hottest pool, the one that was entirely covered by a canopy.

Maybe he could just do his job. He didn't have to coordinate anything with *Annie*. He could do this job himself, and maybe she'd go ask for a different assignment. Anger fueled his steps, and he wasn't even sure why.

He'd dated Carol Anne for six months almost four years ago, and yes, he'd really liked her. Maybe he was even falling in love with her. He didn't know; he'd never been in love before. But the way she'd left like that? Just up and ghosting him?

Of course it had hurt. Logan wasn't a robot, for crying out loud.

He shoved the towels onto the rack with a little too much force, his pulse racing around inside his chest. She did not get to make him feel this way, like he was unimportant and not worth being straightforward with.

Georgia had never lied to him.

*But she had wanted to lie to her family.* The traitorous thought was there, poisoning the very air Logan drew into his lungs.

Thankfully, he didn't see Carol Anne with her dark hair and those long, long lashes. She'd never apologized, never even acknowledged that what she'd done to him was cruel.

He'd told himself that he didn't need an apology, but now that he'd come face-to-face with her, he was thinking maybe he did.

They steered clear of each other until lunchtime, and

when the volunteer coordinator caught him and said it was his turn to go eat, he didn't hesitate. After all, he'd been walking around between two temperatures—hot water and snow—for a few hours now and he was famished.

He went through the line for soup and salad and entered the break room at the back of the small building where people usually paid and rented lockers. It smelled damp and sweaty in here, and Logan wanted to go right back outside.

Instead, he sat down and started eating. There was a strict no-eating policy near the pools, and the tables outside were reserved for patrons.

Back to the towels. Back to avoiding Carol Anne.

He should've known he wouldn't be able to keep pretending like she didn't exist. Because eventually, he ran into her along a narrow strip of cement between the largest pool and the fence.

"Sorry," he said, though he wasn't sure why he was apologizing. She could easily go back the way she'd come too.

"Logan," she said. "Can we talk for a minute?"

He clenched his teeth together and turned back to her, a fake smile on his face. "Sure, you start." He hated feeling petty and small, but that was how she made him feel.

She sighed and tucked her hair behind her ear, like he was being difficult on purpose. Fine, maybe he was.

"I thought you'd have moved on by now," she said.

He laughed, but it didn't contain much happiness or kindness. "I have, Carol Anne."

"You still seem so mad at me."

"I am mad at you," he said. "You disappeared in the middle of the night. I called the police, and it was embarrassing to have to be told that no, you weren't in any danger. It just looked like you'd moved out." His chest heaved, and he worked to control his emotions and his breathing.

"I'm sorry," she said, and everything inside him deflated.

It was amazing what forgiveness could do to a person, and Logan was able to release some of the tension that had kept his muscles tight all day.

She reached up and touched his face, and Logan closed his eyes for a moment, his prayer to the Lord to help him be kind almost over.

When he looked at her again, he felt as calm and as cool as he wanted to be. "I accept your apology."

She flung herself into his arms and held on tight. "Thank you, Logan," she said. "You really are the best." Carol Anne gave him a huge smile and stepped carefully past him, throwing another glance his way after a few steps.

Logan sighed and continued toward his original destination—the laundry. Before he could round the end of the pool, Georgia appeared in front of him.

"Hey," he started, his heart leaping at the wonderful sight of her.

"Who was that?" she demanded, her arms crossed tightly over her chest. It was then that Logan realized how angry she was. He'd seen her like this once—the first time they'd met in the barn, when he'd been holding her hammer.

"That was nobody."

"You hugged her."

He squinted at her. "I guess. That was Carol Anne."

"Oh, your ex-girlfriend," she said without missing a beat.

How she knew that, Logan wasn't sure. Confusion kept him silent a moment too long, because Georgia asked, "Have you been lying to me all this time?"

"What?"

"You said you didn't have a girlfriend."

"I don't. Well, I mean—"

"Maybe you've been cheating on me this whole time." Her voice went up a few degrees. "Seeing her during the week and coming out to the ranch on the weekends. And here I thought you'd been working."

"I have been working," he said.

"I can't believe this." Georgia shook her head, a tear splashing her cheek. She swiped at it, looked at him, and spun away. She marched toward the gate and pushed through it, leaving Logan to wonder what in the world had just happened.

He dropped the used towels off at the laundry and ducked inside the building to call her. When she didn't pick up, he said to her voicemail, "I don't know what just happened. You're my only girlfriend. Can you please call me back?"

## CHAPTER ELEVEN

Georgia swung the hammer wildly at the rafters, knowing she was doing more damage than good inside the still-unfinished barn. But she just needed to hit something right now.

She'd never felt so foolish in all her life. Logan had a hard time getting out to the ranch during the week because of his job. She'd accepted that at face value. Believed everything the man said to her, because he was handsome and fun and the best kisser in the world.

She blinked, and she saw Simon's face as he bent to kiss another woman. Simon as yet another woman hugged him in the grocery store parking lot. All in all, Georgia had discovered that while she and Simon had dated, he'd had no less than six other girlfriends. He hadn't committed to any of them either.

And she was not interested in that kind of relationship.

Her tears threatened to spill down her face again, but she blinked them back. She'd only needed Logan for the holidays, and those were almost over. She had the big Quinn family Christmas soirée at the restaurant, where the gingerbread house winner would be named, and a smaller, ranch family party on Christmas Eve.

She could go to both alone.

After reaching down, she tapped her voicemail icon again and listened to Logan's message. He didn't sound like he was lying—but then again, she'd believed everything he'd said before too.

She didn't know what to believe now.

Sighing, she got off the ladder and picked up the phone. She dialed Logan, knowing he was still at the hot springs, doing his volunteer work. And she'd thought he was so kind and so thoughtful to work while everyone else got into the hot springs for free.

"Hey," he said breathlessly. "I only have a few seconds."

"Oh," she said. She didn't really know what to say to him; she wanted him to talk.

"That was Carol Anne, and we did used to date. But I haven't seen her in years. Please, Georgia, you have to believe me."

She wanted to. She toed the dirt in the barn and said, "All right."

"All right? So I'll come get you tonight like we planned and we'll go to dinner?"

"Yeah," she said, foolishness filling her. Still some anger in there too, but mostly embarrassment for the way she'd acted.

*Now you'll have to tell him about Simon*, she thought as the call ended. She'd told him some things, but not everything. She hadn't thought it important.

She wandered outside to the fence which kept the pigs and llamas from running wild around the ranch. Buzz and Boone loitered nearby, and she leaned against the rungs and said, "You guys have it lucky. Anyone you're interested in is locked up in there with you. You'd know if they were cheating on you."

She stood there for long enough to draw over a few llamas hoping for a treat. When she told them she didn't have anything, they went back to snacking on the hay she'd given them that morning.

They already knew the sad saga of Simon-the-cheater. She didn't need to repeat it to them. But it looped through her mind, and she wished she could somehow purge it.

In the end, she had to go back inside because it was simply too cold to stand outside and talk to livestock.

"Hey," Cami said when Georgia entered the house. "Where have you been?"

"In the barn," she said. If Cami had wanted to find her, she wouldn't have had to look very far.

"I just got the strangest text." Cami got up from the recliner where she'd been reading and approached Georgia in the kitchen. "Look." She handed her phone to Georgia, who looked at the picture on the screen.

It was Logan and that dark-haired woman.

"I've already talked to him about her," she said, handing the phone back. Cami took it, frowning. "But Riley just sent this to me. She said she'd just taken it a few minutes ago."

"No," Georgia said, drawing the word out. "That was at least an hour ago." After all, she'd driven all the way back to the ranch, hammered stuff, and then stood with the animals for a good long while. "Maybe longer."

"But Riley said—"

"Maybe Riley needs to spin her crystals again," Georgia snapped, immediately regretting it. "I'm sorry, Cami. I'm just...stressed."

"I would be too if my boyfriend was cheating on me. Again." She turned the phone toward Georgia. "I just got another one. This time from Ivy. Don't they look like they're about to kiss?"

Georgia stared at the picture, too horrified to take the

phone and examine the image more closely. She lifted her eyes to Cami's, which looked positively sorrowful.

"I'm so sorry, Georgia. Logan seemed like such a nice guy."

Georgia shook her head, unable to keep the tears in this time. No amount of hitting things would help either, she knew. "What do I do?" she asked. She hadn't told anyone about the real reason she and Logan had met, and she was suddenly so glad about that. But it was hard to feel happy with a heart cracking in two.

"You've talked to him?"

"Literally fifteen minutes ago." She sniffed and wiped her face, where every hole there was leaking.

"I don't know," Cami said, the nicest of the sisters. Betsy would've thrown something in Georgia's behalf, grabbed her phone, and sent Logan a nasty message. Jessie would've sat down and made a list of possible solutions and helped Georgia carry out the best one. Georgia herself felt too close to the situation to do anything but stare at the countertop.

"I know what I have to do," she said. "I have to break-up with him."

"Maybe he has a good explanation," Cami said, wringing her fingers together.

"Simon always did too," Georgia whispered, shaking her head. "No. No, I can't do it again. Logan and I are done."

THAT EVENING, WHEN SHE WAS SUPPOSED TO BE GOING TO dinner with Logan, she made sure she was not at the home-stead. Even going to Granny's and Gramps's wasn't enough. He'd stop there if he chose to come out to the ranch.

In the end, she'd texted him the pictures Cami had received and said, *We're done. Please don't come get me for dinner.*

He hadn't responded yet, and Georgia had taken that as an admission of his guilt.

It didn't matter. She'd gone to Granny's and found her about to leave for town, as one of her dearest friends, Maude, had broken her hip a couple of weeks ago. Granny had cookies and buttermilk already in the car, and Georgia rode with them on her lap as her grandmother navigated them toward Quinn Valley.

Honestly driving with a llama behind the wheel probably would've been safer, and Georgia made a mental note to offer to drive on the way back up. After all, it would be fully dark by then, and Granny didn't seem to be able to see very well now, while it was still somewhat light.

If Georgia focused on her phone, she didn't notice how quickly Granny took the curves, nor that she didn't come to a complete stop, well, ever. So maybe she did notice, but at least she could pretend like it didn't bother her.

She pulled up to Maude's house, and Georgia helped carry the cookies and milk up to the front door. Granny went right in, and they found Maude in a recliner, several dishes on the table beside her.

"Look who's here," Granny said as if she were Santa Claus himself. She beamed at Georgia, and that was when Georgia realized she was the real guest here.

"Hey, Maude," she said.

Maude smiled, and Georgia handed the cookies to Granny so she could start to clean up a little bit. She might as well make herself useful, or else she'd find herself on the receiving end of a not-so-fun game of Twenty Questions, and she really didn't need that right now.

She took a handful of dishes into the kitchen and washed them, placing them in the drainer beside the sink, where the others were. Maude probably had her nephew or friends coming by, because it looked like she hadn't moved much since coming home from the hospital.

After opening a few cupboards, Georgia found a trash bag and returned to the living room. She picked up the wrappers and paper towels, grabbed a couple of cups, and left Granny and Maude alone again. Their voices filtered back to her in the kitchen, but Georgia acted like she had so much work to get done.

Really, she'd just gotten a text from Logan that read, *Done? What does that mean?*

Georgia decided to really tell him why those images hurt so much. *My last boyfriend cheated on me for four years. Sorry, I can't do it again.*

She shoved her phone in her pocket when she heard Granny say her name. Maybe she was ready to go already, though Georgia had her doubts. After all, she saw her friends every week, and they never seemed to run out of things to say.

Edging to the corner of the wall that separated the living room from the kitchen, she heard Granny say, "...nice man like Georgia has."

She pulled in a breath. Granny would be so disappointed that Georgia wasn't with Logan anymore. Deciding to be brave, she entered the living room and sat on the couch beside her grandmother.

Maude smiled at her. "How did you meet that Logan Locke anyway?"

"Oh, I hired him to work on the barn." Georgia nodded, feeling dangerous and out of control. "Yep. And to be my boyfriend for the holidays, but that didn't really work out." She flipped a glance in Granny's direction.

Granny barely blinked. "Because you two got along so great, the relationship just took off."

Georgia couldn't really argue with that, but she didn't

want anyone to think she and Logan were still together. And what better way to start the news through the small town of Quinn Valley than to tell Granny and Maude?

"That's true," Georgia said slowly. "But it didn't work out. We broke up today."

That got Granny to blink, and her mouth even dropped open. "But...why? He was perfect for you."

Georgia scoffed, but the sound didn't have much power. "He was not perfect...." For her, or even perfect at all. But she couldn't expect perfection. After all, she knew she wasn't perfect—that no one was. "He was cheating on me."

"Oh, no," Maude said, shaking her head.

"You've talked to him about that?" Granny asked. "I mean, how do you know?"

"Cami has pictures." Georgia thought of her phone, tucked safely away in her back pocket. What had Logan said about the pictures she'd sent? Would he try to deny them? She suddenly felt like crying, like everything she'd tried to piece back together over the course of the last year was about to shatter again.

She took a deep breath, but it shuddered inside her chest. Jumping to her feet, she said, "Excuse me," and headed for the door.

The air outside felt like icy needles in her lungs, but she sucked at it again and then again. She couldn't breathe, and she was certainly falling. Down, down, down somewhere no one would be able to find her.

"Come on, dear." Granny's palm on her back felt like a brand, but it pulled Georgia back from the edge of the cliff. "Come back inside. It's too cold out here."

# CHAPTER TWELVE

*L*ogan shook his phone, like that would make Georgia talk to him. The pictures she'd sent were unbelievable. He'd been at the hot springs, and he didn't experience the same thing those pictures showed.

He just needed to talk to Georgia. Explain everything.

*My last boyfriend cheated on me.*

He wasn't sure she'd even believe him, and that had nothing to do with him. Still, he had to try. He'd texted her half a dozen times since she'd sent the pictures, and she'd gone silent.

So while it was dark, and freezing, he got up and headed for his truck, taking the keys from the hook in the kitchen.

"Where are you going?" Knox asked from the couch in the living room. He had his feet kicked up on the coffee table, but he didn't miss much.

"I have to go talk to Georgia."

"Whoa." Knox jumped off the couch and hurried into the kitchen. He grabbed Logan's arm as he reached for the door-knob. "I wouldn't do that."

Logan looked at his brother's hand and then into his eyes. "Why not?"

"I just wouldn't."

Logan narrowed his eyes. "What do you know?" The need to get to Georgia was almost more than he could stomach.

"She's not at the ranch anyway."

How Knox knew that, Logan wasn't sure. "Then where is she?" He at least knew something, and that was more than Logan did.

"Betsy doesn't know." His eyes widened, and he took a step back.

"Betsy?" Logan asked. "Are you two...dating?"

"What?" Knox scoffed. "No, of course not." But the tips of his ears went red, and he backed up a few steps.

"But you're talking to her," Logan said, advancing. "You have her phone number."

"Yeah, but that's because of work," Knox said, his voice bordering on casual. Almost believable.

Logan didn't have the mental energy to deal with his brother's relationship at the moment. "So, do you know where she is or not?"

"She didn't say."

Logan turned in a circle in the kitchen, trying to find a solution. A road to take. Something that would lead him to Georgia so he could explain. He reached for the doorknob again.

"Are you just going to drive around?" Knox called, but Logan didn't answer. He didn't know what he was going to do.

"Load up," he told Roo and Mortie, and they followed him over to the truck. He opened the door and let them in the cab when they usually rode in the back. He got in beside them, got the truck started, and got the heater blowing.

Then, yes, he just drove around, trying to get his thoughts

to align. If Georgia wasn't at the ranch now, she'd have to come back eventually. Right?

If he drove up to the ranch, would that elevate him to stalker status? Did he want to go there?

Maybe he could just go to the cabin with the gingerbread houses, which he knew was open. The fact that Georgia frequently visited the cabin had nothing to do with it.

Before Logan knew it, he'd pulled under the ranch sign and into the driveway of the cabin that held the gingerbread houses. Lights shone out of the windows of the first two cabins, where he knew her grandparents and her brother lived. Did he dare go knock on their doors and ask after Georgia?

He felt stuck between two rocks, down in a slot canyon, unable to go up or down.

So he didn't get out of the truck and go in to look at the gingerbread houses. He'd seen them all anyway, and he'd have no explanation as to why he was there, other than the truth.

Before he could get out of the truck, a pair of headlights cut a swath through the darkness around him. A car had just turned into the driveway of the first cabin, and his pulse started pinging around inside his chest.

He watched as Georgia got out of the car and rounded the front to help her grandmother out. She walked her all the way to the front door, and then came down the steps to her own car. She got in, the headlights came on, and she backed out, driving right past him while he still sat there.

Logan sat like a sack of potatoes in his truck, utterly confused and in complete despair. He hadn't gotten out. Hadn't said anything.

He'd just sat there and let her pass him. Just like he'd been doing for his whole life. Disgusted with himself that he couldn't seem to *live* his life, only let it happen to him, he pulled out of the driveway and went back home.

❄

A week later, he should've been at the Quinn family party at their family-owned restaurant and pub. He was supposed to be there with Georgia. He'd texted her a few times throughout the past few days, asking if he should still come. She hadn't answered any of his messages, and he wondered if she'd blocked his number the way Carol Anne had.

He'd finished his latest job, and he didn't have anything lined up for a couple of weeks, until the New Year. So he spent some time on the Internet, looking at ranches in a hundred-mile radius, and then headed out.

They did take-out at the restaurant, and he could say he was there for one of their amazing bacon cheeseburgers. Sitting around the house, staring at his phone, wasn't healthy, and Logan had never experienced a darkness like this.

Even when Carol Anne had left town in the middle of the night, he hadn't felt this low. He wasn't sure what that meant, but he knew he couldn't continue like this. Something had to change.

He drove by Quinn's but didn't pull in, hadn't called in an order. He just couldn't bring himself to crash her family party. What would that accomplish anyway?

In the end, he set his truck south and went down the road that had taken him and Georgia to the cookie factory weeks ago. He pulled off on a side road and drove for ten more minutes before coming to his parents' farmhouse.

His mom came out onto the porch, a smile on her face. It was such a comforting sight, and Logan got out and went up the steps to hug her. "Hey, Ma."

"Hi, honey." She patted his back and added, "Where's Knox?"

"Oh, he's out working somewhere."

"What brings you by?" She stepped back and started toward the front door. Logan followed her, glad at the scent of freshly baked bread. "I made biscuits this morning if you want some."

"Yes, please," Logan said, entering his childhood home. He hadn't had a bad childhood, and the familiar curtains actually brought him a sense of peace that had been missing since Georgia's departure from his life.

"What's wrong?" his mother asked, and he should've known better than to think he could show up here and stay silent.

"Georgia broke up with me," he said, sitting at the kitchen table, where butter and honey already waited.

She put a plate of biscuits next to them and sat down beside him. "Oh, baby. I'm so sorry."

"She thinks I cheated on her." He gave his mother a look. "With Carol Anne."

His mom's eyes widened. "Are you serious? Is she back in town?"

Logan nodded. "For a few weeks now. I saw her at the Customer Appreciation Day at the hot springs."

"And why does Georgia think you're cheating on her?"

"Carol Anne and I were assigned to the towels, and after we finally talked the first time, it wasn't so bad. I mean, I don't like her, and we're not getting back together." Logan actually thought he and Georgia could see things all the way to the end. Like, wedding bells end. He hadn't brought it up with her, but the holidays were almost over, and he'd been planning to say something then.

At least that was what he'd told himself, but Logan was starting to doubt he'd have said anything to Georgia, about anything.

"Anyway, I talked to Carol Anne a few times after that, and it was just friendly. I swear, Mom. Nothing is going on between us. But." He pulled out his phone and slid it in front of her. "Her family got these pictures, and they look bad."

His mother picked up the phone and looked at it. "Oh." She put the device down. "I can see why she's upset."

"What should I do?" He picked up a biscuit and split it before slathering butter on it. He left the honey where it was, not being the biggest fan, though this had come from Quinn Organics, which was some of the best in the valley.

"How old is Georgia?" his mother asked.

"Thirty-one," Logan said.

"So she's an adult. You're an adult. Go have an adult conversation with her."

Logan almost shook his head, mostly because he didn't know how to do that. He'd seen her a week ago, the opportunity there to talk to her, and he hadn't taken it. He didn't know how. Didn't know what to say.

"Good idea," he said. "Do you think I just drive up to the ranch and try to talk to her?"

"Yes, Logan," his mother said. "You drive up to the ranch and talk to her." She leaned forward, her own green eyes blazing with energy. "If I hadn't insisted on talking to your father when he was upset with me, you wouldn't be here."

Logan searched her face. "You made Dad mad?"

"Oh, every couple has their trials," she said, waving her hand like the divorce rate wasn't so high in the United States. "But yes, when we were dating, we'd had a couple of disagreements about him being a potato farmer. And I finally drove right out here to this farm and talked to him."

Logan had never heard this story, and it intrigued him. "Like, you didn't want him to be a potato farmer?"

"No, like he didn't think he was good enough for me."

Logan understood the feeling, but he didn't say so. He ate his biscuit, trying to find the courage he needed to drive up to the ranch and face Georgia.

An idea started to form in his mind, and Logan gave his mom a hug before he left.

It took a couple of days for the idea to become a plan, and by the time Logan put his toolbox in the back of his truck, loaded up his dogs, and started for the ranch, he hoped he wasn't too late.

# CHAPTER THIRTEEN

*G*eorgia cleaned out the gingerbread house cabin alone, having volunteered just so she'd have something to do to get her out of the homestead. Robyn had won, of course, almost by a landslide.

The family party at the restaurant had been almost insufferable, but Georgia had survived by sticking close to the table with all the drinks and hanging out with Cami and Ivy. Only a couple of people had asked her where Logan was, and her sister and her cousin had dispatched them on some random task to get them off the subject.

The whole family knew about the break-up now, but it didn't matter anymore. The holiday parties were all over, except for one last ranch dinner tonight. It was only her branch of the Quinn family, and none of them had a significant other, so Logan would've stuck out anyway.

Everyone who'd wanted to keep their gingerbread house had come to get their craft already, and Georgia had said she'd take care of the rest. So the big black garbage bin was full of broken houses, and she'd just finished taking down all the tables. She'd need to borrow a ranch truck to get them back to the party rental store, but she was going to do that after Christmas.

Finished, she pulled her coat back on and headed outside. She'd been to visit the Quinn family cemetery a few times in the past couple of weeks, but she went again. Her favorite headstones were the oldest ones, from many years ago.

"Hello, Grandma-great." Georgia smiled down at the grave marker and kept walking. Her steps were slow, measured, so she could find the things she wanted to say. "How did you and Jerry meet?"

She didn't know all the stories of her ancestors, but she wished she did. She could probably ask Granny, who probably had a half-dozen albums and books that had all the pictures and stories Georgia could want.

Though it was Gramps's family line, Granny was really into the genealogy of the Quinns.

"I bet you didn't have problems," she said to Jerry's head-stone. "Or maybe you did, but you knew how to fix them. I don't know what to do."

Logan had texted several times the first week after their break-up, but he'd stopped after the family party last week.

"It's Christmas Eve," she said to the next buried couple. "Family dinner tonight. I miss Logan." Where those words had come from, she wasn't sure. She hadn't thought them before they'd slipped from her mouth.

But she couldn't make it through another relationship where she was constantly paranoid about where her boyfriend was, or who he was with.

"I should get back to the homestead," she said. "I have a pot of chicken noodle soup to make." She kept her hands deep in her pockets as she held onto the sense of peace and quiet in the cemetery.

She made it to the end of the row and down the next, her breath steaming before her. "Well, I love you guys," she said to her family before making her way to her car parked out front and going back to the homestead.

And she did love her family, though some of them were a bit on the quirky side with crystal healing and palm reading. She supposed she could be considered just as eccentric for the way she talked to dead people and pigs.

Inside the homestead, it was clear both kitchens were being used, as it smelled like bacon as well as pumpkin pie. Rhodes stood in the kitchen with an apron around his waist, mixing the bacon into cream cheese, corn, and garlic.

"How's the corn and bacon dip coming?" she asked.

"Ready," he pronounced with one final stir. He put a lid on the huge measuring bowl and slid it into the fridge to chill. "I'll get out of your hair."

"Thanks, but you can stay." She honestly didn't want to be alone, and Rhodes was actually good company.

"I've got to go help Dad finish the wall in their house," he said, flashing her a smile. "And then I'm going to go down to the entrance and get Grams and Gramps. One of the cowboys told me the llamas and pigs needed more hay."

"All right. I'll take care of them when I'm done here." Georgia put on her own apron and got to work on the soup. An hour later, it was finished and ready, and she escaped the heat of the homestead, which would be full in only another hour.

She stepped onto the back porch and heard one of her beloved pigs oinking. She remembered what Rhodes had said about the hay. Unconcerned, but with a smile on her face, she went down the steps and started toward the pasture where her pigs were.

She was almost there when she heard the hammering. Her steps slowed and stopped, her head swiveling from Columbus the squealer to the doorless entrance to the barn. Maybe she'd imagined the sound, but there it came again.

Strong, steady thwacks of the hammer, from someone who knew what they were doing. Georgia's heartrate picked up at the same rate as her anger. Who was in her barn?

She lifted her chin, her determination filling her. Inside the barn, all her pomp fled at the sight of Logan Locke on the ladder, working to put in the footings for the hay loft.

He wore jeans, a T-shirt, and a vest, as if that clothing was warm enough for winter. He was rugged and handsome, and everything Georgia wanted in her life.

It was as if every experience they'd had together over the past few months streamed through her mind in only a few seconds. She remembered his laugh. How easy the conversation between them had been. How warm his hands were. How safe and secure she felt with him.

How much she loved him.

"What are you doing here?" she asked, nowhere near the bark she'd been going for.

Logan looked at her, his vibrant green eyes drinking her in. "Finishing the job I was hired to do."

"Logan." She didn't know what else to say.

He picked up another nail and added another board to the loft, hammering it surely in place with a few hits. "That woman in the pictures is Carol Anne. We dated about four years ago, and she skipped town in the middle of the night."

Another board, another glance in her direction, more hammering.

"Seeing her at the hot springs was a shock. Did you know I'd actually called the police when she'd disappeared?" He shook his head. "Talk about embarrassing." He continued to place boards and secure them in place.

"The first time we spoke, you were there and saw it." He looked right at her. "I've never lied to you. There is nothing between Carol Anne and me."

Georgia found herself nodding, because he spoke in a strong, sincere voice. "Cami had pictures," she said.

Logan climbed down off the ladder and put the hammer on the workbench. "I realize that. But they're innocent. Once she'd apologized, we talked a little bit. She gave me a hug for forgiving her. Nothing, and I mean *nothing*, is going on with her." He took a few steps toward Georgia. "I've never lied to you, and I've never cheated on you. Georgia." He took her hands, and she was too numb to do much more than think. "Georgia, please believe me."

Logan was here. Finishing the barn. Saying all the right things—and she did believe him.

"Georgia, I'm in love with you, and I'll do anything I have to in order to get you back." He gazed down at her, and she felt the truthfulness of his words all the way down in her toes.

"Tell me what to do, and I'll do it," he said.

"Well," she said, swallowing. "First, you're going to kiss me, and then we're going to finish this barn."

# CHAPTER FOURTEEN

*L*ogan couldn't believe talking to Georgia had been as easy as it had been. He knew they still had some things to work out, but as he bent his head toward Georgia, he thought he could handle whatever discussions they still needed to have.

He touched his lips to hers gently, seeking permission, and she sighed into him. Encouraged by what she'd said and her reaction, he kissed her again, holding on longer and really letting her know how he felt.

He did love her. He wanted her to know, and while he'd said it, there was nothing like *feeling* it.

The best part of this whole scenario was that she kissed him back. She hadn't said those three little words, but Logan felt them way down in his soul.

When he finally came to his senses and pulled away, he felt like he was complete again. "I'm really sorry," he whispered.

"I know you are." She opened her eyes, those beautiful hazel pools he loved so much. "I am too. I over-reacted, I know that. I do. I just...." She trailed off, and Logan pressed his forehead to hers.

"You don't have to explain." He'd never had anyone cheat on him before, and he wasn't quite sure he could imagine it, but he was trying to give her the benefit of the doubt. Trying to imagine how he'd feel if she'd been unfaithful to him behind his back.

He couldn't quite envision it, and he was glad for that, but he could try to be empathetic and kind to her as she worked through some things.

She exhaled and backed up, tucking her hands into her coat pockets, glancing around. "Logan," she said. "You've been here longer than a day."

"Every day this week," he said. "I'm almost done." In fact, the loft and the ladder up to it were all that remained. "I wanted to finish it for you for Christmas. Then I was going to come knock on the door and tell you."

Her eyes met his. "How did you do this without me knowing?"

He chuckled, his eyes tracing all the things he'd finished, from the shelves along the door, to the door itself, to the almost-finished loft. "I honestly don't know. That hammer is loud, and I haven't tried to be quiet. Rhodes caught me on the first day."

"Rhodes?" She faced him again.

"Yeah, he said he wouldn't say anything."

"He told me the animals needed more hay down here." She strode through the door to the fence. "He's such a liar." She returned to the barn, her eyes flashing with that fire Logan liked so much.

"You think he told you that to get you down here?"

"That's exactly what I think." She smiled and started laughing, and Logan did too.

She sobered and turned toward the doorway again. "I

haven't come out to see the pigs for a few days," she said. "They reminded me too much of you, actually."

"Oh, now no one wants to hear that." He laughed again, stepping over to her. "I did a door here that slides," he said. "Instead of swinging open and closed. Takes up less space, and I thought the shelves here would be nice for feed or equipment or supplies."

"They are nice." She leaned into him. "I suppose you want to know about Simon, right?"

"Only what you want to tell me, sweetheart." Logan had no idea how to help Georgia, but he'd do his best.

"Maybe another day," she said. "It's Christmas Eve, and I just want to enjoy it with my boyfriend."

Logan had never heard better words, and he went with Georgia as she moved back outside to her beloved pigs and llamas. They stood there until she said she was cold, and then he went into the homestead with her.

He'd only been here a few times, and once it had been full of people. The other times, he'd just picked her up and they'd left. But today, she gave him the full tour, including her office, which screamed about her organization and obsession with things being straight and even. Now that he knew her better, he understood her need to ensure that everything lined up just-so.

She wasn't perfect, but what she could control, she tried to make that way.

Logan wasn't perfect either, and he stood in her office, wanting to give her the world. "When my mom and dad were dating, they had a fight," he said. "My dad knew he was going to be a potato farmer, and that life wasn't exactly what he thought my mom wanted."

He wasn't sure why he was telling her this, only that he wanted to know where she really stood. "I don't even have a potato farm, Georgia. Look at this office. Look at what you have. I can't give you any of that."

"Of course you can," she said.

"How do you think I'm going to do that? Rhodes is going to inherit this place. Maybe his new wife will want to run it. Or he will. I mean, I know what you do is valuable." Logan paused for a moment, some of his insecurities and fears coming out in his voice.

"Maybe we should buy a ranch of our own," she said. "I know that's what you want, Logan."

"I'm scared," he admitted.

"Sometimes we have to take a leap of faith," Georgia said. "You don't even know if you can afford a ranch, because you've never gone and talked to someone."

"Dinnertime!" a woman called, and Logan turned from the doorway. The other Quinn siblings started filling the kitchen, along with their parents, and Rhodes came in a moments later with his grandmother and grandfather.

With just the nine of them, plus him, they could fit at the regular dining room table, and Logan stood back and watched as everyone started putting their culinary contributions on the counter.

Rhodes had made corn and bacon dip, much to his grand-father's delight. Betsy, the self-proclaimed chef, had done a brown-sugar glazed ham, while Cami had made a cheesy scalloped potato to go with it. Georgia had crafted chicken noodle soup, and Logan knew what he'd be eating. And Jessie had made honey wheat bread.

It wasn't classic Christmas fare—well, maybe the ham was —but it was exactly what Logan expected from this family. He loved them all, and he could hardly believe he might have a shot at becoming one of them.

"Logan," Betsy said with more surprise in her voice than he thought necessary. "What are you doing here?"

"Oh," Georgia said, stepping out from behind the kitchen counter. "Everyone, Logan and I made up. He's here for dinner." She beamed at him, and Logan could only smile back, especially as everyone welcomed him back.

Her mother stepped over to him while he waited in line and said, "It's good to see you, Logan."

"Thank you, ma'am."

"How's your mother?"

"Doing great."

"You know she and I play bunko every month, right?" The way Georgia's mother looked at him, Logan had a feeling that something very significant was being said.

"I did not know that." He picked up a slice of bread, which still felt warm. "Seems like you'd know how she's doing if you see her all the time."

"Yes, well, we've been worried about you and Georgia."

Logan ladled soup into his bowl. "Are you telling me... what are you telling me?"

"My family likes to meddle," Georgia said. "It's usually Granny, but I have to say, Mom, you've done a fine job."

"I do not meddle," she said, her voice a bit haughty. "I simply suggested to Lucy that she talk to you about...talking to Georgia."

"To be fair," Logan said. "Georgia is a little scary." He whispered the last few words, which caused her mother to laugh and Georgia to say, "Hey."

"I'm kidding," Logan said. "Kind of." He ginned at her and took a seat at the table next to Betsy. "So are you and Knox dating?"

"What?" She scoffed. "No." She was much better at fibbing than Knox, as her face didn't even turn red. "He's the farrier and I see all the cowboys when they come to the homestead for meals." She immediately turned to Jessie and asked her something, so Logan let the subject drop. At least for now.

After dinner, he and Georgia cuddled on the couch, and he thought about looking up some more ranches, really doing the leg work he needed to in order to have all the facts. "I think I'm going to go talk to someone about buying a ranch," he said. "At least then I'll have all the information and can make an informed decision."

"I like that idea," Georgia said.

Logan did too.

*Six months later:*

"I don't know," he said, the Idaho summer wind pulling at his cowboy hat. He put one hand on top of his head to keep the hat in place. "Which one do you like better?"

Georgia, hatless, squinted out at the horizon, which was still the ranch they'd come to visit. "I like this one best," she said. "Number one, it's still in Quinn Valley, and number two, it's bigger."

"The homestead needs a lot more work," he said. "And did you see that yard?" He shook his head. This wasn't anything like Quinn Valley Ranch, with its sprawling green lawns and perfectly manicured roads. Even the gravel stayed where it was supposed to on her family's ranch.

"So we'll fix it up." She put her arms around him. "Together. It has more cattle, and there's even a pasture for all my llamas."

He chuckled though part of him was still nervous. "It's the pigs you care about, sweetheart. Don't think I don't know that."

"We'll have to build a barn for them," she said. "They have a lot of special dietary needs."

Logan grinned at the gently waving grasses, this patch of earth something he could afford and something where he and Georgia could build their family, their future, together. "I think I know how to build a barn," he said.

"Then I think you—*we*—should get this one."

Logan had wanted to have somewhere to call his own before he and Georgia took the next step in their relationship. That, and she needed more time to really trust him. They both needed time to understand that their relationship was real and could be lasting.

Logan knew it could be, and if he could get this ranch, he thought he might finally have everything he'd ever wanted.

But he needed her too, so he turned toward her and asked, "So this one?"

"This one." She gazed up at him and smiled.

"And Georgia?" he asked.

"Yeah?"

"How do you feel about getting married?"

Shock paraded across her face, especially when Logan dropped to his knees and started fumbling in his pocket for the ring he'd carried with him everywhere for the past two months. "I think we should start some of our own family traditions," he said. "And there's no one I want to do that with other than you. Will you marry me?" He held out the ring, hoping the wind didn't try to steal it from his fingers.

She stared at it and then him, finally taking a breath. "Yes," she said as she exhaled. "Yes." The second time she said it, the word was practically a shriek. She squealed and laughed as Logan slipped the ring onto her finger, got to his feet, and kissed her.

"I love you," he said.

"I love you too, cowboy."

❄

Read on for a sneak peek of **SECRET SWEETHEART.**
It's available in paperback!


And keep reading to get the coveted Quinn family recipe for corn and bacon dip! Serve it at your next family gathering...or for dinner. Whatever. :)

# CORN AND BACON DIP RECIPE

## Corn and Bacon Dip

1 pkg. cream cheese
1 c. sour cream
¼ c. mayo
2 garlic cloves, minced
¼ t. hot pepper sauce
1 can corn, drained
1 lb. bacon, cooked and crumbled

COMBINE EVERYTHING. COVER AND REFRIGERATE FOR several hours. Stir again. Serve with your choice of crackers or vegetables.

# SNEAK PEEK! SECRET SWEETHEART CHAPTER ONE:

*B*etsy Quinn drew in a deep breath, the scent of brown sugar, maple, and the salty ham filling her nose. It was the best smell on the planet, and she couldn't help bending down to smile at the meat candy currently baking in the oven.

The kitchen at the farmhouse buzzed with activity, as the family Christmas Eve dinner was about to start. She smoothed her hair off her face and glanced at the timer on the oven. She had twenty minutes before the ham needed to be basted again.

She could easily run out to the blacksmith shop to see Knox. She tried to push the idea away, but it already had her heart beating a little faster, and while the kitchen radiated heat, the temperature inside her was what spiked.

Everyone seemed busy enough. She could sneak away. After all, Georgia already had, and her chicken noodle soup sat on the back burner of the stove, just taking up space.

"Rhodes," she said, turning to her brother as he got something out of the double-wide refrigerator. "Do you need me to go get Granny and Gramps?"

"No, I'll go grab them. I need to get my presents from my cabin anyway." He barely looked at her. The only time Betsy found the spotlight among her family was during mealtimes. It shouldn't matter so much to her, but providing good food and getting complimented on it really meant something to her.

Betsy backed up a step, almost expecting Cami to say something to her. Ask her where she was going. Something. Her younger sister didn't even look her way.

So Betsy spun on her heel and hurried into the mudroom off the side of the kitchen. She shoved her feet into a pair of snow boots that were two sizes too big and put on her coat. She hustled outside as she zipped it up, because she only had a few minutes.

The glowing, yellow lights in the buildings on the ranch brought a sense of comfort to her she hadn't known she needed. She'd felt unsettled these past few months, and in the quiet moments before she went to bed, she allowed herself to admit the exact date everything in her life had been put in a blender and then turned on high.

The day Knox Locke had been hired at Quinn Valley Ranch.

She'd immediately gotten his number, as she had all the ranch hands' numbers. She texted them in a group so they'd know if she'd have lunch at the homestead that day or not. She'd been immediately entranced by his dark green eyes, a more subdued version of his twin's.

Betsy's steps slowed. She couldn't date her sister's boyfriend's brother. Could she?

*Probably should talk to Georgia about it*, she thought. But she didn't turn back, and Georgia was going through a tough time with Logan right now anyway. They weren't exactly together anymore, and Betsy's heart took courage.

If Georgia wasn't dating Logan, she had no reason to object to Betsy starting something with Knox.

But every step Betsy took along the cleared path toward the blacksmith shop testified of something different. Pushing aside the doubts, she stuck her hands in her pockets, hoping for a bit of warmth. December in Idaho possessed a kind of icy brutality that pockets could not stave off.

*The blacksmith shop will be warm.* The thought drove her to move faster, and as she approached, she slowed. She felt like someone had tied her to a yo-yo in October, when Knox had shown up on the ranch wearing that delicious gray cowboy hat and saying he was their new farrier.

She'd texted him and asked him what he was doing for Christmas, and he'd said he had a ton of work to do for the new year since he was leaving town for a couple of weeks immediately following the holiday.

*After that,* he'd messaged. *I'm going home for dinner.*

He hadn't asked her to come visit him. He never did, but Betsy felt fireworks between them every time they were in the same room together. And it was time to find out if Knox did too.

"If he doesn't, fine," she whispered to herself, her breath steaming into a thick cloud in front of her. "You'll find someone else." That statement was ridiculous, as Betsy rarely left the ranch and hadn't dated in...she couldn't even remember how long. She went to church with her family, and she'd met a man here and there over the years.

But nothing had ever sparked as hotly as the flame between her and Knox. As evidenced by what had happened in the kitchen, her excitement for him grew just by thinking about him.

Still, she stood at the door of the blacksmith shop without going in. Would he think her too forward?

*Now or never*, she thought, the cold pressing down on her now. The tips of her ears would be frostbitten if she didn't either go into the shop or hurry back to the house. She checked her phone—only twelve minutes left before the timer on her ham went off, and someone would know she'd snuck out.

She raised her hand to knock, deciding to be brave and really pound on the door. Her fist swung down at the same time the door opened, and she ended up punching Knox in the face.

He grunted and groaned and fell back a couple of steps. Both of his hands went to his face, and horror struck Betsy behind the ribs.

"Oh, no," she said. "I'm so sorry." Blessed warmth emanated from the shop, and she rushed forward to help him. "I'm sorry, Knox. I was just knocking to see if you were here."

"I'm here," he said through his fingers. He touched his nose, and his fingers came away blood-free. He inhaled and sniffed and met her eye.

Those fireworks went off, and Betsy stilled. The man before her had never indicated that he liked her for more than the woman who fed him sometimes. Perhaps there had been a moment or two over the past two and a half months where his gaze had lingered on her. Maybe an extra smile. Some late-night texting.

Or maybe she'd hallucinated those instances because she'd been crushing on him since his arrival on the ranch.

"Ready for your trip?" she asked, mentally kicking herself for such a stupid conversation topic. She was thirty-four-years-old, and she should be better at flirting with a man. Letting him know that she was interested, so that the ball was in his court.

"Yep," he said with a slow smile. "How's the party prep coming?"

She glanced at her phone again. "I have about nine minutes before I have to be back." She took a step closer to him. "I just thought...." She couldn't finish, because she had no idea what to say. Or what she'd been thinking.

Foolishness raced through her, and Knox obviously had more experience with relationships than she did, because he said, "I was just heading out. Want to walk back up with me?"

"Yes," she said, relief raging through her. She flashed him a tight smile and kept her hands clenched into fists in her pockets.

"What did you make for dinner?" he asked, following her out of the shop and turning back to lock it.

"Maple and brown sugar glazed ham," she said. "We all make our own dishes, and they somehow come together into a meal."

"Sounds nice," he said.

"You could stay," she said, immediately wanting to glue her lips together. She already knew he was going to his parents' house. They'd already talked about this.

Knox looked at her, a curious edge in his eyes that could barely be seen through the thickening darkness. "I'm going to miss you while I'm gone." He smiled at her, and the walk back to the house happened with clouds beneath her feet.

"Have fun on your cruise," she said as she paused with her foot on the bottom step.

He chuckled, the sound rumbling through her chest in the best possible way. "Yeah, me, my brother, and my parents. Going to be a real riot."

"Is Logan going?"

"He was," Knox said. "But then a job came up. So no, not this time."

Betsy nodded, her smile seemingly stuck in place. "See you when you get back."

"I hope so," Knox said, and Betsy seized onto that hope and took it with her back into the homestead.

She'd just hung her coat on the peg when the timer went off. She darted around the corner and pulled her ham out of the oven. She basted the meat and ran a knife along all the slices.

"Dinnertime!" she called, and people got up from the couches and came into the kitchen. While she'd been gone, Rhodes had gone down the road to the cabins near the entrance, and Granny and Gramps shuffled forward to survey the food spread on the counter.

Wheat bread, chicken noodle soup, scalloped potatoes, and ham. And of course, Rhodes's corn and bacon dip. Betsy had given up the argument that an appetizer wasn't really part of the meal, because Rhodes didn't care what she thought—at least about this.

"Hey, Granny," she said, linking her arm through her grandmother's.

"There you are, dear," she said. "I didn't see you when I got here."

Betsy's whole body flushed. *I'm going to miss you while I'm gone.* "I ran outside to say good-bye to a friend," she said just as a man moved in front of her.

"Logan," Betsy said with a healthy dose of surprise in her voice. "What are you doing here?"

"Oh," Georgia said, stepping out from behind the kitchen counter. "Everyone, Logan and I made up. He's here for dinner." She beamed at him, and Betsy welcomed him back even as her heart sank all the way to her toes. Maybe all the way into the floor.

They'd made up. She should be happy for her sister—and she was.

But it put her and Knox on fragile ground again. Thankfully, her mother engaged Logan in a conversation, sweeping him away from Betsy so she could allow the smile to slip from her face.

Everyone started serving themselves, and Betsy stood back the way she always did during mealtime. "Want me to get you something, Granny?"

"Soup and ham," she said. "And that bread, and as much dip as will fit on the rest of the plate."

Betsy giggled and picked up a plate and a bowl for her grandmother. "It's no secret what you like," she said, shaking her head.

"Well, some secrets are worth keeping," Granny said. "And some aren't." She picked up a napkin and the silverware she needed.

Betsy looked at Granny and then focused on ladling some soup into her bowl. "What are you saying?"

"Was that Knox I saw leaving just before you came in?"

"I didn't come in," Betsy said, the lie bitter on her tongue. She glanced down the line, but Gramps was behind Granny, and he was still buttering a slice of Jessie's honey whole wheat bread.

Her eyes met Granny's again, and the older woman just smiled. "Oh, okay. I see how it is." She touched her lips in the universal sign of a secret. "It'll be our little secret."

"I appreciate that," Betsy said, almost under her breath. "It's just...."

"I know what it is," Granny said after a few seconds of silence. "Like I said, some secrets are worth keeping, and some aren't. Maybe this one is, at least for a little while."

Betsy finished loading the plate with the food her grandmother wanted and took it to the table for her. She returned to the line and got herself some food before sitting down. Logan, of all people, sat right beside her and picked up his fork.

"So are you and Knox dating?" he asked, point blank.

"What?" Betsy scoffed though a path of worry burned through her with the speed of a racecar. "No." She laid her napkin on her lap. "He's the farrier and I see all the cowboys when they come to the homestead for meals."

She turned away from him, her heart hammering in her chest. Had he seen her and Knox outside too? Had Knox said something to him? Jessie sat on her other side, and she said, "Hey, Jess. How's that new software working?" Her sister managed the herd, the pregnancies, and the sale of cattle, and she'd just gotten a new tracking system a few weeks ago.

Jessie answered, but Betsy honestly didn't hear her. Granny's words drifted through her mind. *Some secrets are worth keeping.*

So she'd keep her crush on the gorgeous Knox Locke a secret. No problem. She could do that.

Couldn't she?

**Grab <u>SECRET SWEETHEART</u> in paperback** and keep reading in the Quinn Family to see if Betsy can get her cowboy happily-ever-after!

**Contracted Cowboy (Book 1):** A fake ad brings a cowboy to Georgia's door just in time for all the Quinn family holiday parties, so she hires Logan to be her boyfriend. Nothing can go wrong with this plan...except she might lose her heart to her newly contracted cowboy.

**Secret Sweetheart (Book 2):** She's a domestic goddess. He works on her father's ranch. They could have forever...if they could take their relationship out of the shadows. **Can she overcome her anxiety and fear and build a life with Knox? Or will their relationship be doomed to die in the shadows at Quinn Valley Ranch?**

**Landscaping Love (Book 3):**
He hired her to landscape the yard, but she's going to make him re-evaluate who he lets into his heart. **Can Rhodes and Capri landscape their love? Or will they go their separate ways once the yard is finished?**

**Birthday Boyfriend (Book 4):** This Quinn cowgirl doesn't need a lot for her birthday...just the cowboy she's been crushing on for months. Will Flynn ever see Jessie standing right in front of him?

**Fall Fireside (Book 5):** Cami Quinn has had enough of being the shiny new date for the cowboys in Quinn Valley. She's on her fifth or sixth broken heart, and she needs the soothing, healing messages she's found at the fall fireside series in the past. Will Cami and Clay find a way to mend what's broken inside themselves in order to find a happily-ever-after?

# ABOUT LIZ

Liz Isaacson writes inspirational romance, usually set in Texas, or Wyoming, or anywhere else horses and cowboys exist. She lives in Utah, where she writes full-time, takes her two dogs to the park everyday, and eats a lot of veggies while writing. Find her on her website at feelgoodfictionbooks.com